JESSAMINE'S FOLLY

SUZANNE G. ROGERS

IDUNN COURT PUBLISHING

CONTENTS

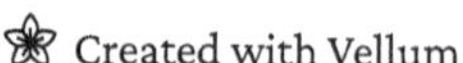 Created with Vellum

Dedicated to my romantic husband, Robert.

*"Love is the wisdom of the fool
and the folly of the wise."*
~ Samuel Johnson

CHAPTER 1

MISFORTUNE

NOVEMBER, 1902. DERBYSHIRE, ENGLAND.

S wathed in a black veil, Lillian sat alone in the back of the church. As young Jessamine Foster made her way up the aisle after the funeral service, pale and forlorn, Lillian's heart bled. When Jessamine passed by, her gaze lingered on Lillian's face. Startled, Lillian averted her eyes and bowed her head—as if in prayer. *I've never regretted my decisions before—until now. If circumstances were different, I would take her into my home and give her the world.* Even at age fifteen, the girl showed signs of great beauty and good breeding. After her debut in three years, she could make a splendid marriage. *Any connection with me would spoil her chances.*

Moments later, Jessamine's Uncle Thackery followed Jessamine from the church. Next came Thackery's wife Rachel and daughter Charlotte—who appeared to be about Jessamine's age. Certainly the Fosters would look after Jessamine and make sure her launch into Society was managed well. *I can be a silent benefactor, at least. The poor girl will want for nothing, and be comforted in the knowledge she has someone who cares—even if we never meet.*

1

MOURNERS POURED into Arbor Manor after the double funeral for Jesse and Minerva Foster, clad in black and wreathed in sorrow. Numb, Jessamine barely heard their expressions of condolences, although she forced herself to nod and express gratitude like her parents would have wished. Fortunately, the staff did an impeccable job serving refreshments, so she didn't have to worry about playing hostess. Jessamine's aunt seemed to warm to the task, however, although her high-handed manner with the servants set Jessamine's teeth on edge. Cousin Charlotte apparently had gone straight to her room after the carriage returned from the cemetery, since she was nowhere to be seen. Occasionally mourners would glance at Jessamine, shake their heads and whisper things like, "Orphaned at such a tender age, poor girl."

Mr. Abernathy, the family attorney, murmured she was to join him and her uncle for a few moments. Like a puppet on a string, she followed him into the library, where he shut the door. Mr. Thackery Foster was already there, standing with his back toward the fireplace. *How like Papa he is in little ways, and yet not like him in the essentials.* Jessamine sank onto a sofa and tried to listen as Mr. Abernathy explained her financial situation, but his words seemed to be coming at her from a great distance. After his meaning finally sank into her brain, her grief turned to shock. "My father's entire estate is entailed away from me? Surely he made some provision for my future."

"I'm afraid not," Mr. Abernathy said.

"As his attorney, did you not advise him he wouldn't live forever?"

"Repeatedly, Miss Foster. Several months ago I suggested setting aside a sizable dowry on your behalf, but he kept missing our appointments to sign the papers." He shook his head. "This is a terrible tragedy in so many ways."

Panic set in. "Where am I to go?"

"Rest assured, you're welcome at Arbor Manor as long as you like," Mr. Foster said.

"That's very gracious of you, sir," Mr. Abernathy said. "Don't you agree, Miss Foster?"

Although Jessamine opened her mouth to speak, only a strangled sort of moan emerged.

"You and your cousin Charlotte are very close in age," Mr. Abernathy said. "I daresay you'll be like sisters."

The very notion curdled Jessamine's blood. *I cannot bear Charlotte's company for ten minutes! How are we to live under the same roof?* Blinking back tears, she returned to the drawing room. As she glanced around the elegantly appointed space, taking in its magnificent woodwork, crystal chandeliers, and oriental rugs, her gaze settled on the huge oil painting of her family hanging over the fireplace. *No doubt that will be the first thing to go.*

WITH CRITICAL DETACHMENT, Mrs. Foster watched as two footmen carried Jessamine's family portrait from the drawing room and toward the staircase. "Don't gouge the walls with that horrible thing."

Upon hearing her aunt's voice, Jessamine emerged from the library. Her heart sank as she watched the footmen struggle to lift the unwieldy painting up the staircase. The Fosters had moved into Arbor Manor only two days prior, and already Mrs. Foster was making changes.

"Oh, there you are, Jessamine," Mrs. Foster said. "The maids are moving your parents' clothes and personal effects into the attic. Whatever you don't want, we'll box up for charity. The poor are grateful for any old rag."

"Yes, Aunt."

"Oh, and Charlotte would like a room with a balcony. Since yours is the only one that suits her, you must choose another on the third floor."

A prickle of heat traveled down Jessamine's spine. "There are fifteen bedrooms in this house, and several of them have lovely views of the garden. Surely Charlotte will be content with one of them."

The tight smile on Mrs. Foster's lips never reached her eyes. "The sooner you realize this is *our* house now, the better. Your uncle has been generous enough to give you a place to live and food from our table. You should be grateful."

"I *am* grateful—to my uncle," Jessamine retorted. *Your good fortune is at my expense, and you're not even gracious about it!*

Mrs. Foster's nostrils flared. "I'll thank you to keep a civil tongue in your head."

Jessamine's cousin appeared on the landing just then, clad in an off-the-shoulder silk gown with a floating skirt of white tulle. "Mama, isn't this the most beautiful dress you've ever seen?"

Delighted, Mrs. Foster clasped her hands together. "Oh, don't you look gorgeous!"

Jessamine gasped. "Where did you find that dress? You can't have it!"

As she descended the stairs past the footmen, Charlotte's smirk lent an ugly cast to her pretty face. "Why not? It was hanging in one of the spare rooms, and everything in this house belongs to Papa now."

"Not exactly. That was the dress my mother wore when she was presented to the queen," Jessamine said. "I was to wear it for my debut."

"You're not to have a debut anymore, so I should have it." Charlotte's smug tone was insufferable. "Don't be so selfish, cousin."

Jessamine spoke through gritted teeth. "Take it off right now."

"Mama?" Charlotte pleaded. "Make her see reason."

"Charlotte is right, Jessamine," Mrs. Foster said. "You won't have a Season, so you don't need the gown. Think about someone else for once in your miserable life and let her have it."

As her aunt spoke, something inside Jessamine snapped. She advanced on Charlotte with her fists clenched at her side. "Take it off or I'll *make* you take it off."

"Jessamine Anastasia Foster, how dare you speak to Charlotte like that!" Mrs. Foster exclaimed.

Mrs. Foster fluttered in the background as the two girls glared at one another for several long, hostile moments.

"Fine," Charlotte said finally. "I won't wear it then."

She reached across the bodice, grasped one of the puffy gossamer sleeves, and gave it a vicious tug. The fabric and the trim ripped, sending beads raining to the floor. The next thing Jessamine knew, her hand flew out and slapped Charlotte across the face. The footmen had reached the landing at that point, but nearly dropped the painting as they craned their necks to watch the conflict. Her cousin and aunt shrieked, but Jessamine brushed past them and mounted the stairs.

"You're a wicked girl, Jessamine Foster!" Mrs. Foster exclaimed.

Furious, Jessamine paced in her room until she grew calm enough to think. *My only regret is in not slapping Charlotte*

harder! Although her overwhelming impulse was to flee the house and never see the Fosters again, she had no refuge available to her, and even fewer resources. *Why did Mama have to be an only child?* As her temper cooled, Jessamine began to feel slightly more remorseful. *My parents did not raise me to act like a hoyden. I can't allow Charlotte to goad me into unladylike behavior!*

When a brief thump came at her door, Jessamine opened it to discover her mother's gown thrown in a heap in the hallway. Biting back tears, she hung the dress up, averting her eyes from the damaged sleeve. *I must collect the trimmings!* She ran downstairs, dropping to her hands and knees on the floor to retrieve as much of the scattered beads as she could find. Miss Hannah Yates, her lady's maid, found her sitting on the bottom step several minutes later, sobbing and clutching a handful of trim.

"I heard what happened." Hannah's tone was soothing. "Let me have those beads. Maybe I can repair the dress."

Jessamine poured the beads into her palm. "Thank you. I'm not sure how I can go on like this."

"You'll stand it as long as you must, Miss Jessamine. One day at a time."

Mrs. Foster intercepted the young footman as he moved through the entryway with a silver salver. "Is that the post, Eugene?"

"Yes, Mum. I was looking for Mr. Foster."

"He's out on business. Just leave it in his study."

The footman disappeared into the nearby study and emerged a few moments later with the empty silver salver. Mrs. Foster busied herself arranging a vase of flowers in the entryway. After Eugene disappeared downstairs, she went into the study to examine the post. An assortment of bills and correspondence were of no interest, but then she came upon a letter to Jessamine with no return address. The envelope was subtly scented with expensive perfume and bore a London postmark. Intrigued, Mrs. Foster slit the envelope open and unfolded the letter. To her astonishment, three twenty-pound notes were tucked inside. She read the message written on the heavy stationery, and a chuckle escaped her lips. After she slipped the money into her pocket, Mrs. Foster crushed the letter and envelope, tossed them into the embers of the fireplace, and left the study.

She located Eugene as he was polishing silver in the servant's hall. When she appeared, he scrambled to his feet. "Anything I can do for you, Mrs. Foster?"

"Eugene, you bring in the post every day, do you not?"

The footman nodded. "Yes, mum."

"Miss Jessamine has an unwanted admirer who continues to send her the most unsettling letters. Whenever there's any correspondence for her without a return address, I'd appreciate it if you would give it directly to me."

"Only the letters without a return address?"

"Yes, that's it. The poor child has had enough upset, wouldn't you say?"

"Oh, yes, mum."

Mrs. Foster pressed a guinea into his hand. "No need to say anything about this conversation to anyone, least of all Miss Jessamine."

Eugene's eyes bugged out at the money. "No, Mrs. Foster. I understand you perfectly."

As Mr. Foster was seated at the dinner table, he frowned at Jessamine's empty chair. He hesitated before dipping his spoon into his soup. "I don't like all this brouhaha. Should I send for the girl, do you think?"

"No, I've had the footmen move her and her things to a room on the third floor, and she's to take all her meals there from now on," Mrs. Foster said.

"I don't care if she ever comes down," Charlotte said. "She slapped me and I'll never forgive her."

"Jessamine shouldn't have done so, but by all accounts you provoked her, Charlotte," Mr. Foster said. "You should have asked Jessamine's permission to wear the dress first."

"What would have been the point?" Charlotte shrugged. "She would have just refused."

"Your cousin lost her parents, her estate was entailed away from her, and she's grieving," Mr. Foster said. "Perhaps tearing her mother's dress wasn't the most cordial thing to do."

"She'd no right to fly into such a rage," Charlotte said. "It was an accident."

"That's right, it was," Mrs. Foster said. "I saw the whole sordid episode. Now that I know her temperament, I wish Jessamine had some other place to live."

"We can always put her to work in the kitchen." Charlotte snickered.

"Or as a scullery maid," Mrs. Foster said.

Mr. Foster shook his head in exasperation. "Let's have no more of that talk! Mr. Abernathy suggested I set aside a reasonable sum for Jessamine's dowry. It seems the least I can do."

"Absolutely not!" Mrs. Foster said.

"You've already done too much by letting her stay here, Papa," Charlotte said. "It's embarrassing, having a poor relation hanging about."

"Mr. Foster, let me assure you that giving Jessamine a dowry is a wasted gesture," Mrs. Foster said.

"I don't quite take your meaning," Mr. Foster said.

"She has no money, no connections, and won't be invited anywhere."

"Jessamine is my niece and a Foster! And, might I add, she's a very pretty girl indeed."

"Her prettiness is of a common sort. The streets of East End are strewn with pretty girls just like her."

"Mrs. Foster!"

Undeterred, the woman continued. "No gentlemen of distinction will have anything to do with her. Her expectations have been ruined, and by giving Jessamine a dowry you'll raise her hopes cruelly."

Mr. Foster peered at his wife. "So now a dowry would be cruel, would it? I cannot imagine you have her best interests at heart."

"Why should I? Jessamine and her mother lorded their good fortune over us all these years."

"They did not!"

Mrs. Foster shrugged. "Whatever you say. I, for one, find your inheritance quite satisfactory."

"Me too," Charlotte said.

UPSTAIRS IN JESSAMINE'S tiny third-floor bedroom, her dinner tray sat cooling on a small wooden table pushed up against the wall. Although she'd never realized it before, a ventilation grate in the wall allowed her to hear all conversation in the dining room quite plainly. As Mrs. Foster, Charlotte, and Mr. Foster began to make plans for the three of them to visit

London over Christmas without her, Jessamine dropped her face in her hands and wept. Among all the other things that had happened, her sixteenth birthday had come and gone and nobody had said a word.

CHAPTER 2

THE JOURNEY

JANUARY, 1905

As Jessamine pulled white sheets off the trunks and wooden chests stacked in the attic, her eyes began to water and she could not hold back a sneeze. Hannah passed her a handkerchief.

"Bless you, Miss Jessamine. It's certainly dusty up here."

"Thank you." Jessamine sniffed and blotted her eyes. "And it's wretchedly cold, too. Why don't you ask Eugene and Lawrence to bring my mother's trunks down to my room? We can sort through the clothes there, where it's warmer." Her gaze fell on a keepsake box of her mother's, and she gave it a pat. "Have them bring this, too."

"Yes, Miss Jessamine."

"I certainly hope her things fit me. We've can't let the hem down on this dress any further, and the bodice is so tight as to be scandalous."

"What doesn't fit, we can alter," Hannah said. "Don't fret."

Mrs. Foster's shrill voice floated up the attic stairs. "Jessamine!"

Hannah and Jessamine exchanged a terse glance.

"I'll be right down, Aunt Rachel," Jessamine called out.

Hannah gathered several hatboxes into a pile, while Jessamine descended the attic stairs and joined her aunt in the third-floor hallway. Mrs. Foster wrinkled her nose at Jessamine's disheveled appearance.

"You've cobwebs in your hair," she said.

"Surely that's not why you wished to speak with me?"

Mrs. Foster's lips thinned out, and she thrust a newspaper into Jessamine's hands.

"I've circled several governess advertisements appropriate for someone of your status. You're nineteen, and there's no reason you can't earn your own living."

As Jessamine took the proffered newspaper, apprehension knotted her stomach.

"Charlotte, your uncle, and I will be leaving for London at Easter, and I want you settled before then."

"I'll begin answering advertisements right away," Jessamine replied. *Anywhere is better than here.*

Mrs. Foster turned on her heel just as Hannah came down the attic stairs with an teetering stack of hatboxes. Jessamine tucked the newspaper under her arm and helped carry the boxes into her room. "It seems I'm to become a governess," she said, trying for a tone of nonchalance. "My aunt insists I leave the house as soon as possible."

Hannah gasped and her eyes widened. "Oh, no!"

Despite her best efforts not to cry, a tear ran down Jessamine's face. "I suppose it was inevitable."

"I'm sorry, Miss Jessamine." The maid lowered her voice. "Forgive me for being so forward, but I'm shocked you've been treated so shabbily, and by your own family too."

"I absolutely forbid you feeling sorry for me." Jessamine swallowed the lump in her throat. "It's not like I'm not the first woman of reduced circumstance forced to seek a living, and I won't be the last."

"I'll ask the staff if they've heard of any open positions. Most of us have relatives in service, so you never know."

"I'd be very grateful." Jessamine opened one of the boxes and peered inside. "Now let's see what damage time and moths have wrought."

DALLAS MARSDEN, Seventh Earl of Kirkendale leaned against the arena fence and watched his stable master exercise a young stallion named Folderol. The horse reared up on his back legs, nearly dislodging Trask in the process. When Folderol failed to remove his unwelcome rider, he broke into a flat out run and then braced his legs. Although Trask was an expert horseman, he flew over the horse's head to the ground and lay still. Alarmed, Dallas climbed the fence and hastened to the man's side. "Are you all right? Is anything broken?"

The man groaned, but a slight smile found its way to his lips. "Looks like I just put the fall into Folderol."

Chuckling, Dallas helped Trask to his feet. At the same time, the beautiful stallion cantered around the arena, snorting. A couple of groomsmen ran alongside, trying to catch hold of Folderol's bridle. When the horse eluded them, Dallas laughed. "I'm beginning to think the horse has a bit of the devil in him."

"That he does, milord, but we'll tame him by and by."

An unwelcome voice drew Dallas's attention. "Lord Kirkendale! Good afternoon."

Speak of the she-devil.

Dallas turned to see Olivia Hightower in full riding habit, atop her mare, Dresden. He lifted his hand in greeting, but he could not have been less pleased. *The woman always seems to be a harbinger of bad tidings.* As he made his way to the arena gate, Olivia urged her horse over to meet him.

"Dallas, I heard your governess resigned."

"What?"

"Yes, I passed a hired carriage on the way here, and your butler informed me just now Miss Bartlett was in it."

Dallas scratched his head. "She was the fourth one this year alone, and they never stick around long enough to tell me why they leave."

"I think her departure was due to illness in the family or some such thing." Olivia paused. "Listen, I'm always running to town. You should let me take your sister shopping. She's going to need a great many gowns for her debut."

"That's kind of you," he said. "Thank you for calling, but if you'll excuse me, I must speak with Amelie." *Ha! If I discover my sister has had anything to do with chasing away the governess, I shall threaten her with Miss Hightower.*

JESSAMINE SAT ON HER BED, exploring the contents of her mother's keepsake box. The cedar box contained photographs, mementoes, old letters, and the family Bible. One photograph of two beautiful girls caught her eye. Their arms were around each other's waists, and their heads were bent together as if they were the best of friends. On the back of the image was the inscription "Me and Aunt Lillian—the toasts of London." *Aunt Lillian?* Her mother had never spoken of having an aunt, much less one who appeared to be about her age.

Among the letters, Jessamine found several packets of correspondence from a Lillian Perrisham. *That must be Aunt Lilly!* She skimmed a few of the oldest letters, which were full of news about social gatherings and gossip. Curiosity prompted Jessamine to examine the family Bible. Sure enough, Lillian was the youngest daughter of Jessamine's great-grand-father, born just one year before Jessamine's mother. There was no date of death, she noticed. *Did Mama and Lillian have a falling out, or had Mama simply forgotten to write in the date?*

Jessamine picked up the photograph and went in search of Mr. Hattley, who'd been the head butler at Arbor Manor for as long as she could recall. He was in the wine cellar, taking inventory.

"Mr. Hattley, I was wondering if you'd ever met Lillian Perrisham, my mother's aunt."

When she held up the photograph, his eyes lit up. "Ah, yes, I remember her. I'd just come to work here after you were born, and she was a guest. Miss Perrisham doted on you."

"Do you know what ever happened to her?"

"I don't know the particulars, but as a butler you tend to hear certain things. I believe your great-aunt fell in with a fast crowd. I never saw her back here after that."

The wave of disappointment following his words caught Jessamine off-guard. She'd hoped to discover a long-lost rela-tive who would welcome her with open arms. Instead, she'd unearthed a potentially unseemly connection who hadn't even bothered to send a condolence card after her parents' death.

"You favor her, if you don't mind me saying so," Mr. Hattley said.

Jessamine peered at the photograph. "I hadn't noticed before, but you're right. We could almost be sisters."

Hannah appeared at the door. "I thought I heard your voice, Miss Jessamine. Amos is waiting to speak with you, if you have a moment. He may have a lead on a position."

"I'll come right away." Jessamine smiled at Mr. Hattley. "Thank you for your help."

She left the butler to his tasks and accompanied Hannah to the servants' hall. The middle-aged groundskeeper was waiting with his hat in hand.

"Hello, Amos," Jessamine said. "Hannah said you might have some information for me?"

The man nodded his head. "Aye. My cousin Garfield is valet to the Earl of Kirkendale. He wrote me just the other day about the young lady of the house needing a governess, or companion more like, since Lady Amelie is turning eighteen soon. The thing is, no governess has managed to last at Knight's Keep more than a few weeks."

Jessamine blinked. "Is the girl difficult?"

"The problem might lie with the master of Knight's Keep. Lord Kirkendale is Lady Amelie's elder brother, and the Earl of Kirkendale since his father died. It seems no lass young enough to be a governess or companion to Lady Amelie can avoid falling in love with the man. He's that handsome, says my cousin."

"What a bunch of ninnies!" Jessamine exclaimed.

"Aye. Well, you know how impressionable young women can be. Anyway, Lord Kirkendale is looking to fill the post. It's likely only a temporary position, however, until Her Ladyship makes a good marriage."

"I think I can avoid falling in love until then," Jessamine said. "I'll send Lord Kirkendale an inquiry immediately."

"I'll ask my cousin to put in a good word for you. Garfield has His Lordship's ear."

"Thank you, Amos. All the newspaper advertisements my aunt circled are for positions in India or South Africa. If I must work, I'd rather it be in England."

If only to spite Aunt Rachel.

~

THREE WEEKS after Mrs. Foster's ultimatum, Jessamine rose before dawn to prepare for her journey to Knight's Keep. After she dressed in a traveling suit and Hannah had helped arrange her hair, she examined her reflection in the mirror. The hem of the trumpet-shaped skirt had been let down a half inch, the plain bone buttons on the bolero jacket had been replaced with smart new ones made of jet, and a pleated lace cuff had been added to lengthen the sleeves.

"It's funny, but I can remember Mama wearing this suit when we traveled to London," Jessamine said. "It's not too much out of fashion, is it?"

"With the changes we made, it's splendid," Hannah said. "And your mother would be proud to see what a beautiful young lady you've become."

"I'm glad we saved so many of Mama's clothes and shoes. If it had been left up to Aunt Rachel, they'd all be gone by now and I'd have to dress in rags."

"It's not my place to say so, but you've not had a new garment since your parents died, while Mrs. Foster and Miss Charlotte deny themselves nothing. It's a scandal."

"If I dwell on it, Hannah, I'll go mad." Jessamine reached under the pillow on her bed, pulled out a package, and handed it to Hannah. "This is for you. I can't thank you enough for all you've done."

The young maid unwrapped the paper and discovered a jeweled hatpin. Hannah's inhaled gasp of delight made Jessamine smile.

"It was my mother's, as I'm sure you know. She would have wanted you to have it."

Hannah let out a sob. "Thank you so much. I'm going to miss you something fierce, Miss Jessamine. I pray you'll land on your feet."

As the two women embraced, Jessamine felt tears sting the backs of her eyelids. "I don't know what I'll do without you. You've been such a comfort."

"I'll always be here to help you if I can."

"Bless you. I'm determined to do well as a governess. If Lady Amelie marries quickly, this first position may not be long. At least I'll have a reference for the next one."

"I'm sorry for everything that has happened, but I know you'll do well at whatever you turn your hand to."

"You've always been so kind." Jessamine took a deep breath. "I suppose this is good-bye."

"I'm afraid none of the family is up yet to see you off."

"I didn't tell any of them that I was leaving today, and I doubt they would have bothered to see me off at any rate. I did leave a note for Uncle Thackery in his study, should he bother to look." The lump in Jessamine's throat grew larger, and she could hear the strained quality of her voice. "I'm not sorry to be going. These past three years have been the worst of my life."

After the women exchanged another quick embrace, Jessamine fled the room and crept downstairs to meet the chauffeur in the chilly courtyard. She tried not to look back as the rig drove away, but she couldn't help herself. Oddly enough, without her parents in residence, the beauty Arbor Manor possessed seemed hollow to her now.

AT THE TRAIN STATION, Jessamine bought a ticket to Kent with money her uncle had given her for Christmas, and sank down on one of her trunks to wait. The veil on her hat helped her ignore the curious glances of passersby who might wonder why a young, unmarried girl was traveling unaccompanied.

A porter took charge of her trunks when the train arrived,

and Jessamine stepped on board. She was fortunate to find an empty compartment, so she settled in and ate the breakfast the kitchen staff had insisted she take with her. Although she hadn't thought she was hungry, the fruited muffins and flask of tea were welcome. At first the food had a calming effect, but as the miles sped past, her doubts and anxiety increased. *What if the earl and his sister don't like me, or what if I don't like them? If I'm discharged for any reason, where am I to go?* She had a few pieces of her mother's jewelry she could sell in a pinch, but then what? Hannah had shown her a few things with a needle and thread, so perhaps she could become a seamstress if no other governess positions presented themselves. *I'll never take money and family for granted again!*

Her correspondence with Lord Kirkendale had revealed him to be, on paper at least, an intelligent man who expressed himself well. What Amos had told her about the unsuccessful string of governesses, however, had given her pause. Had the ladies truly embarrassed themselves by setting their sights on His Lordship, or was he actually a serial seducer who discharged the women directly after making his conquests? Of course, it was equally possible they'd been let go for refusing the man's advances. Since she'd been forewarned, she would be on her guard.

Slashes of crimson marked Mr. Foster's cheekbones as he strode into his wife's sitting room with a piece of folded stationery in hand. "Jessamine left early this morning to take a position as a companion, but I've no idea where. The chauffeur informs me he drove her to the train station before breakfast."

An expression of delight transformed Mrs. Foster's counte-

nance. "What marvelous news! Now we may prepare for Charlotte's upcoming Season in peace."

Mr. Foster tossed Jessamine's note into his wife's lap, on top of her embroidery hoop. "I've let my elder brother down by failing to take care of his daughter. Where on Earth did Jessamine get the idea she should seek employment?"

"I encouraged it, of course."

The flush marking Mr. Foster's cheekbones spread over his entire face. "Forgive me for saying so, madam, but your attitude toward Jessamine is and always has been extraordinarily callous. If the situation were reversed, I've no doubt my brother and his wife would have done everything in their power to take care of Charlotte, and would have treated her like their own daughter."

"You're upsetting yourself unnecessarily. Jessamine is better off where she is."

Mr. Foster's eyes narrowed. "A young girl is traveling alone to God knows where, friendless and unprotected, and yet you express no concern for her well-being? Mrs. Foster, you'd best hope no harm falls to Jessamine, or I'll never forgive you."

CHAPTER 3

KNIGHT'S KEEP

Dallas felt a pang of regret as Trask led a beautiful chestnut colt from the stables. The horse's hot breath showed white against the chilly morning air as the stable master tied its reins to the back of an empty rig. "I'll be back afore long, milord."

"Take all the time you need," Dallas replied. "We want Gaston to arrive at his new home in good condition."

The stable master picked up the reins and urged his horse forward, while Gaston swished his tail in anticipation of the exercise. Dallas ran his hand across the colt's glossy flank as he walked past and gave the horse a final pat. Amelie would at least be spared the ordeal of watching the colt leave. Dallas was glad, since his younger sister was tender-hearted.

His stomach growled in anticipation of breakfast. Dallas tore his gaze from the departing rig and strode across the frost-encrusted lawn toward the house. To his dismay, he spotted his pretty younger sister streaking toward him with her long dark hair unbound. *The best laid plans of mice and men just went awry.*

Amelie's boots slipped on the moist grass as she drew near, and her arms pinwheeled. Dallas caught her under the arms before she fell. "Whoa...steady! What are you doing up so early?"

Her cornflower blue eyes stared at him in accusation. "I saw Trask leaving just now with Gaston. You didn't sell him, did you?"

"I'm afraid so."

"Oh, Dallas, how could you! Joséphine will be so lonely now."

"We can't keep every horse we breed, Amelie. It wouldn't be practical."

Her lower lip trembled. "I don't care about being practical. I care about Joséphine. She'll miss Gaston terribly."

"Horses aren't the same as people, Amelie. Besides which, I explained to Joséphine her offspring is going to live on Sir Bartholomew's estate, where he'll meet lots of pretty fillies. She was quite contented."

Despite her brother's lighthearted jest, Amelie frowned. "Don't be ridiculous. I'm not a little girl anymore. And I don't understand why you sell all our best horses to Sir Bartholomew. He doesn't deserve them."

Dallas merely smiled, linked his arm with Amelie's, and steered her back toward the house.

"Miss Foster is arriving today, isn't she? Tell me again, why do I have to have a governess?"

"Consider her a companion, then. Miss Foster will accompany you to shops and such so you can prepare for the Season. You must admit, I'm perfectly useless in that regard."

Amelie pouted. "What makes you think Miss Foster will be any different than any of the others? You always discharge them after a few weeks."

"I don't discharge them; they run off for one reason or

another. At any rate, Miss Foster comes with a very good reference. Besides which, we've gone through every other governess in the country, so let's hope she works out." Dallas gave his sister a droll look. "If not, Miss Olivia Hightower has offered to take you under her wing."

"I'm sure she'd love that, as long as you're part of the bargain. The woman has made no secret of her intentions."

"I know you don't like her, but Miss Hightower would make a suitable wife." He tried to keep the distaste from his voice.

"Oh, Dallas, you don't like her, either! Don't you want to fall in love?"

"Romance and love are for young girls, Amelie. Any marriage of mine will be based on facts, not emotion."

"I can't understand how you can be so hard-hearted."

"Plenty of practice, dear sister."

AFTER JESSAMINE REACHED LONDON, she was obliged to hail a hansom cab to ferry her and her luggage from King's Cross to Victoria Station for the last leg of her journey. As she gazed out at the exciting, bustling streets of London, she grew wistful. *Had Mama and Papa lived, we would have moved into our Eaton Square townhouse in a week or two, and paid dozens of social calls. Invitations to teas, brunches, balls, and soirees would have arrived, and we would have accepted as many as possible. Perhaps Mama and I would have ridden on Rotten Row and greeted our new friends and old acquaintances. And I would have danced all night long until my slippers wore out...*

She wrestled her tortured thoughts away from ghosts and memories and focused instead on how she would handle her first meeting with Lord Kirkendale. *What if I don't suit him and he sends me home immediately?* The thought of returning to Arbor Manor in disgrace was inconceivable. *I won't give Aunt Rachel or Charlotte the satisfaction!* No matter what, Jessamine was determined to fit in to her new position.

When her train arrived at the Canterbury East Railway Station, it was mid-afternoon. A porter hailed her a cab, and as the driver loaded her trunks he asked for her destination.

"I've come to work for Lord Kirkendale. I'm his sister's new companion."

"Aye, I was told to be on the lookout for ye. Knight's Keep is but five miles from here."

The driver clucked to his horse, and the cab began to move. A flurry of bumblebees began swirling furiously inside her middle, and her fingers grew cold. *I've never been so scared to meet anyone before. Please don't let me faint at the earl's feet!*

Completely absorbed in *The War of the Worlds* by H.G. Wells, Dallas frowned when his butler stepped into the library to announce a visitor.

"Miss Foster has arrived, milord."

"Ah. Show her in, Mr. DeVane, and send someone to locate Lady Amelie."

"Yes, sir."

"And bring tea," Dallas said.

"Right away, sir."

As the butler ushered Miss Foster into the room, Dallas stood. The woman was taller and seemed far younger than he'd anticipated, with large blue eyes set in an oval face. He could not tell her hair color with complete certainty because it was hidden underneath a hat, but a brunette lock had escaped its pins and was curled against the back of her neck. The dark color of the traveling suit she wore rendered her ivory complexion almost translucent, but her cheeks had no bloom. A quick glance at the woman's hands revealed they were shaking with fear. *Why, Miss Foster resembles a trembling, skittish kitten, and seems very little older than Amelie!* His heart sank; his sister needed a strong personality to keep her in check, not a fluttering, pale girl with oversized eyes. Still, it would be unfair to dismiss the new governess before she'd had a chance to speak.

"Please sit, Miss Foster," he said. "Thank you for coming. I'm Dallas Marsden, Earl of Kirkendale."

"It's a pleasure to make your acquaintance, Lord Kirkendale. I look forward to meeting Lady Amelie."

To his pleasant surprise, her voice was melodious and cultivated. Dallas felt Miss Foster's eyes on him. He expected her to look away when he met her gaze, but to his surprise she did not. *Not so skittish after all?* Instead, she lifted her chin and gave him a serene, if somewhat forced, smile.

"I understood from your letter that the loss of your parents had led you to seek employment?" he asked.

"Both succumbed to a sudden illness, I'm afraid, a little over three years ago. I've been living with my uncle and his family since."

"Both parents at once? What a terrible blow." He paused. "My own father passed away two years ago, and my mother has been gone a year now. One never completely gets over the shock."

"No, I expect not."

Amelie tore into the library at full speed, bare-footed. She leaped over a needlepoint-covered oval footstool, and skidded to a stop in front of Miss Foster.

"*Je viens de voir la chose la plus horrible dans le grenier!*" she exclaimed. (I just saw something horrible in the attic!)

His sister then reeled off a torrent of French so fast Dallas could only catch every third word or so. *The little minx! Her French was always better than mine.* Amelie gesticulated, pointed toward the ceiling, and made exaggerated expressions of fright. Miss Foster had a mild look of surprise on her face, and Dallas was certain she hadn't understood a word. He opened his mouth to explain the best he could, but before he could say anything, Miss Foster spoke.

"*Pardonnez-moi, Lady Amelie, mais c'est plutôt impoli de parler français quand votre frère n'a évidemment vous comprends pas,*" she replied. (Forgive me, Lady Amelie, but it's rather rude to speak French when your brother obviously doesn't understand you.)

Taken aback, Amelie gaped.

"And I don't believe in ghosts—in the attic or anywhere else," Miss Foster added.

Dallas suppressed a smile at Amelie's scowl. *Touché.*

"Miss Foster, allow me to introduce my sister, Lady Amelie," he said. "I believe Amelie was attempting to impress you with her grasp of French."

"And a most excellent display it was," Miss Foster said. "Your accent is impeccable, Lady Amelie."

"As is yours, Miss Foster," Dallas said.

As the maid brought in a tea cart and proceeded to pour, Miss Foster fixed her gaze on Amelie. "You must enjoy scary stories?"

"I adore scary stories."

"There's an American author by the name of Edgar Allan Poe who writes some formidable ones. You should read *The Tell-Tale Heart.*" She lowered her voice, as if to impart a secret. "It's about a man who commits a murder."

Amelie's mouth hung open. "Really?"

"My papa used to say my reading of it sent a chill down his spine."

"I'm quite fond of a good scare myself," Dallas said. "Perhaps we could hear you read it aloud? I believe I have Poe's complete collection of works."

"How splendid!" Miss Foster said. "I'll look forward to it very much."

As she sipped her tea, Jessamine hoped nobody noticed the nervous trembling of her hands. Her arrival at Knight's Keep had been inauspicious; although the butler had been cordial at first, after she told him she was Lady Amelie's new companion, he quickly became brusque. Thereafter, she'd been so unnerved by her introduction to Lord Kirkendale, she could barely speak. Lady Amelie's sudden entrance, however unorthodox, had allowed Jessamine the chance to regroup. Although the girl's intention had been to embarrass her with a rapid volley of French, Jessamine was pleased she'd managed to turn the tables nicely. After Jessamine's years of tutoring, there was little Amelie could do to trip her up...except have an older brother whose golden good looks were dreadfully distracting. *But I'm not a ninny, and I needn't behave like one.*

Jessamine cleared her throat. "I saw several beautiful horses grazing in the pasture upon my arrival. Do you enjoy riding, milady?"

Her face lit up. "I'd ride every day, if I could."

"Good. That will give us something to do together, if His Lordship doesn't mind."

"Not at all," Kirkendale said. "Trask, the stable master, will be happy to accommodate you."

Jessamine took her first deep breath since she'd arrived,

and allowed her shoulder to relax. Evidently, she was not to be sent away—yet. "Thank you."

"If you've finished your tea, Miss Foster, I'll have someone show you to your room so you can settle in," Kirkendale said. "Dinner is at seven."

~

A MAID ESCORTED Jessamine to her room. Along the way, Jessamine admired the beautiful gaslight fixtures. "Is there no electricity in the house?" she asked.

"Since Knight's Keep was at one time a castle, the thick stone walls pose a challenge to the electrician."

Jessamine's bedchamber was not overly large, but it was well appointed. Several tapestry hangings softened the harsh edges, a fireplace stood ready to provide warmth when required, and her four-poster bed proved comfortable enough when she took a moment to test it. Her trunks had already been brought to her room, so she occupied herself hanging up her gowns.

The Fosters will have discovered my absence by now. Aunt Rachel and Charlotte will be celebrating, undoubtedly. The note Jessamine had left for Mr. Foster had been perfunctory and dispassionate. Without mentioning the name of her employer or an address, she'd written only that she'd accepted a companion position. Admittedly, her uncle had not been wholly unkind, but he was very often in London and almost never intervened when Aunt Rachel treated her harshly. Would he give her departure a second thought? *Probably only to rejoice there would be no more friction between me, Aunt Rachel, and Charlotte.*

Her meeting with Lord Kirkendale and his sister had gone well enough. Although Amos had apprised her of the young earl's dashing appearance, her first glimpse of the man had taken her aback. *Perhaps I've led a sheltered life, but I've never seen such a magnificent man before.* Snug breeches had revealed the long lean muscles of his legs, and his jacket was tailored to his athletic frame beautifully. His nose was perhaps a trifle too broad for classic good looks, but it balanced out his wide mouth in perfect harmony. The disarming hazel eyes gazing at her from beneath his strong brow seemed to lay her soul bare... until she reminded herself who she was and why she'd come. *It makes no difference if he resembles Quasimodo or Adonis. I'm a servant now.*

She found it significant Lord Kirkendale had received her in the library and not the drawing room. The man obviously felt more comfortable and easy surrounded by his books than the ordinary trappings of wealth and status. And what a library it was! Although many estates featured rooms filled with expensively-bound volumes, ordinarily the books were only for show. Lord Kirkendale had been reading just before she met him, however, judging by the book on the table next to his chair. Albeit reluctantly, Jessamine had to admit the man appeared to be thoughtful and well-read, not the shallow pleasure-seeking aristocrat she'd been anticipating. *But first impressions can be deceiving. I can't drop my guard.*

Jessamine laughed as she recalled Amelie's naughty behavior; it hadn't been anything out of the ordinary for a high-spirited girl, but imagine trying to frighten her away with a silly story about a ghost in the attic—in French no less! *I like her already, and I hope she will come to like me.*

WHEN THE DINNER dressing gong rang, Jessamine donned a plain, high-necked gown with an onyx brooch pinned at her throat. With no maid for help, she was obliged to twist her hair into a simple coil and pin it in place with the help of a comb. As she descended the stairs, her heart began to beat faster. *It's not too late for Lord Kirkendale to send me away. Please let me get through the evening without embarrassing myself!*

At the base of the stairs, she glanced around, hoping to discover where the drawing room was located. A young footman passed by with a drink-laden tray.

"Excuse me, but could you tell me where to find the drawing room?" she asked.

His lip curled. "You're the new governess, aren't you?"

"I'm Lady Amelie's companion, Miss Foster."

"The name's Carter. I'm heading to the drawing room now. Follow me."

With a smirk on his face, the footman led her toward an open door just off the entryway. As Jessamine approached, she heard the low hum of conversation. *Is the earl having guests?* When she entered the room, she discovered perhaps a dozen fashionable people assembled. *Oh, no, I'm too plainly dressed for a party!* Several guests stared outright, and some of the ladies snickered behind their hands. One of the older gentlemen leered openly at her face and figure.

Lady Amelie was perched in a window seat across the room. When she caught sight of Jessamine, her eyes widened and she shook her head. Confused, Jessamine took a few steps in Amelie's direction, but she was quickly intercepted by her brother. In his black tail coat and white bow tie, Kirkendale was easily the most handsome man in the room.

"Good evening, Miss Foster. May I help you with something?"

The question seemed an odd one, and she wasn't quite sure how to respond.

"I-I'm sorry, but I thought dinner was at seven."

"And so it is. Why don't you wait in the entry hall? I'll ring for someone to show you to the schoolroom, where your meals will be served."

Jessamine's stomach dropped, and her face and neck flamed hot with embarrassment. She managed a curtsy and a murmured "Forgive the intrusion, sir," before her retreat. Titters accompanied her exit, and as she paced outside the drawing room, she could overhear the aftermath of her inappropriate appearance.

"That was my sister's new governess," Kirkendale said. "She was lost."

A lady's voice reflected amusement. "For a moment, I thought she meant to dine with us! A governess may be a necessary evil, but she can't be trusted to stay in her place. You'd best beware, Dallas."

Jessamine gasped. *Is that what they all think of me?*

"You're quite right, Miss Hightower," said a man's voice. "Every governess I ever knew tried to worm her way into marriage to the man of the house or to his son or brother."

"You'd think the poor creatures would know better," Miss Hightower replied.

Horrified, Jessamine backed away from the door. *If Lord Kirkendale believes I will try to worm my way into his affections, he'll be very sadly mistaken!*

"She's a companion, not a governess." Lady Amelie sounded annoyed. "And since Miss Foster has only been at Knight's Keep a few hours, I doubt she's formed a design on Dallas."

"Let's not quarrel, dear," Miss Hightower said. "It's your birthday after all."

Nobody mentioned it was Lady Amelie's birthday! When Carter emerged from the room a few moments later with his empty tray at his side, Jessamine bristled at him.

"That was a nasty thing for you to do," she whispered. "You could have warned me."

"Well aren't we all high and mighty? You asked for the drawing room and I showed you the drawing room. It's not my fault you made a fool of yourself."

Chuckling, the footman ambled off. Although Jessamine gritted her teeth against her rising temper, the lion's share of her anger was reserved for Kirkendale. *Why didn't he tell me earlier where I was to take my meals if it was not to be with the family?*

Lady Amelie scampered from the drawing room. "Dallas sent me to show you to the schoolroom. I begged off dinner with our stuffy neighbors and we're to eat together."

"Are you sure? I heard it's your birthday celebration."

"They won't miss me and I won't miss them. Come on."

CHAPTER 4

THE PICNIC

Lady Amelie showed Jessamine down the hall and into a spacious room. One corner of the room had been set up as a classroom, with several easels, a large chalkboard, a desk, and a bookshelf full of chalk, pens, ink pots, and slates. On the other side of the room was a sitting area and a fireplace.

"This is where I had most of my lessons growing up, but I suppose I should ask Dallas if I could make it over into a sitting room now," Amelie said.

"I'm horribly embarrassed about what just happened," Jessamine said. "The governess in my family always took meals with us, but I suppose we were an odd case. Thinking back on it, perhaps that's why Miss Riley cried so hard after my parents died and my aunt discharged her."

"Don't give it another thought. My brother's guests are horrid people. They may be our neighbors, but I don't care for their company."

Maids came into the schoolroom to set the sitting room table for two and to serve the first course—a shrimp cocktail.

"Thank you for dining with me, milady," Jessamine said as she picked up her fork. "It's very gracious of you."

"I confess, I was planning to play a few more tricks, but you'll be happy to know I've abandoned my plan completely. Tonight was punishment enough."

"Indeed it was."

"It also occurred to me if I don't make you completely welcome, you'll run off and I'd be stuck with Miss Hightower to get me ready for the Season. She's at the dinner party tonight and would like nothing better than to marry my brother."

Although Jessamine did not remember Miss Hightower's face from her brief sojourn in the drawing room, she couldn't forget the woman's sly insinuations. *Best to change the subject and think of something more pleasant!*

"Let's you and I go riding tomorrow," Jessamine suggested.

A genuine smile of pleasure curved Amelie's lips. "I'd enjoy that very much. I'll show you all my favorite places on the estate."

"Do you suppose the cook would pack a picnic lunch for us? It's several weeks shy of spring, but we've been having gorgeous weather lately. We'll have a little birthday party of our own."

"What a marvelous idea! I haven't had a picnic in ever so long," Amelie exclaimed. "I'll send word to Mrs. Crandall to have something ready."

As Jessamine ate, part of her was still trapped in the drawing room, feeling scorned and embarrassed. Even though she had no money now, she was still a gentleman's daughter— perhaps not equal in rank to the people who'd laughed at her, but at least worthy of their notice. A wicked twist of fate had stolen all that away from her, however, and nothing could be done about it. *And damn Lord Kirkendale for thoughtlessly exposing me to ridicule. If there is any benefit to be gained by the entire debacle, it would be my diminished opinion of him!*

Seemingly eager for female conversation, Lady Amelie bombarded Jessamine with questions about the latest fashion trends in hair, clothes, music, and literature. As the meal progressed, Jessamine enjoyed the conversation—which inevitably turned to Amelie's upcoming Season. *If she is to make her debut at the same time as Charlotte, I will do everything in my power to make sure Amelie outshines her.*

"Is it true I'll be expected to play the piano in front of people? I'm not used to playing for anyone other than my music teacher or brother," Amelie said.

"I can't wait to hear you play the piano. It will be good practice, and girls who can play or sing are always held in high regard."

Amelie's pert nose wrinkled. "I'd always imagined my debut as wonderfully romantic, but Dallas makes marriage sound like a business transaction. Among the many qualities he's looking for in a wife, apparently love isn't one of them."

Inwardly, Jessamine squirmed. The extraordinarily handsome earl could very well be the sort of gentlemen who planned to have a string of devoted mistresses at his beck and call in addition to a loyal wife—but she would never dream of saying so to his sister.

"Just because His Lordship doesn't believe in romance doesn't mean your admirers will feel the same way," Jessamine said. "You must hold out for the very best, milady. You deserve to fall madly in love, and be loved in return."

"And you, Miss Foster? Do you aspire to a romantic marriage?"

"I did have hopes in that direction, but when my financial circumstances changed, I decided to never marry." *And you may convey my sentiments to your brother!*

"How terribly sad."

"Despite my decision, it doesn't mean I don't wish differently for others. In fact, being witness to true love is the most wonderful thing in the world. My parents were proof of that."

"I'm not sure my parents were ever in love." Amelie's expression lost its usual vivacity. "They were quite distant with one another, you see."

"Perhaps they chose to keep their affections behind closed doors?"

Amelie's thin shoulders moved in a shrug. "Papa was posted to the British embassy in Paris, and lived there most of the time. *Maman* was born in France, but she lived here with Dallas and me. She was sad most days, and I think she was lonely. I believe her unhappiness affected my brother's opinion of marriage."

Jessamine brushed off an unexpected twinge of sympathy for Kirkendale. *His feelings are not my concern.* She focused on London, and spent the rest of the meal talking about all the delights Amelie could expect once she'd arrived. After they were finished eating, one of the maids returned to clear away the dishes from dinner.

"Milady, His Lordship bids you come down to the drawing room to join his guests."

"Oh, thank you, Maureen," Amelie said.

"Miss Foster is invited as well." Maureen's tone was decidedly cooler.

Ha! If Angel Gabriel himself summoned me to Lord Kirkendale's side, I would refuse to go! "That's very kind of His Lordship, but I believe I will retire," Jessamine said. "I've had a long day traveling."

Amelie pouted. "I was hoping you would read that story about the telling heart."

"*The Tell-Tale Heart.* Some other time, milady. His Lordship's guests would doubtless find it tedious. But we'll meet at the stables tomorrow, like we planned. Would ten o'clock suit you?"

"Oh, yes! I'll look forward to it."

Amelie left and Jessamine slipped upstairs to her room. Without the girl's uplifting presence, Jessamine's resentment and wounded pride at the way she'd been treated earlier resurfaced. *Never mind. Today has been horrible, but tomorrow will be better.*

WHILE HIS GUESTS played an animated game of charades, Dallas stood in the back of the room nursing a snifter of brandy. When Amelie entered the room and hastened to his side, he gave her a smile.

"I hope you enjoyed dessert," he whispered. "Mrs. Crandall did a magnificent job with your birthday cake."

"I had two slices, thank you, since Miss Foster didn't eat hers," Amelie whispered back.

His eyes flickered to the doorway. "Your governess didn't come with you?"

"*Companion.* Miss Foster said she was tired, but I know better." Amelie poked a finger at his chest. "You let people be mean to her."

"I did not!" Despite his denial, Miss Foster's embarrassment had weighed heavily on his mind throughout dinner. "Not intentionally, at any rate."

"Miss Foster and I are going riding tomorrow afternoon, and we're bringing a picnic with us."

"A picnic? Am I invited?"

"No," she teased.

"How cruel."

A giggle escaped Amelie's lips. "It's no more than you deserve. Anyway, I like Miss Foster, and I don't want you to chase her off."

"I'll try to be on my best behavior."

Olivia glanced over her shoulder at Dallas and patted the empty place next to her on the sofa. "Come now, don't stay to yourself. Join the game!"

Although he gave her a polite smile of acquiescence, inwardly he groaned.

Dawn was glimmering through the east-facing windows when Jessamine awoke. She rose to check the weather through the deep-set leaded pane glass windows. The spring day looked perfect for riding. After she donned her riding habit, Jessamine sat at her vanity table to arrange her long locks. She wrestled with the thick tresses for a time until she finally braided it, coiled the length, and pinned it in place at the nape of her neck. *Hannah could always work magic with my hair, but I must now learn to manage by myself. I should have paid more attention when she was arranging it!*

A place setting for one had already been laid when Jessamine arrived in the schoolroom, and she remembered Amelie would be having breakfast with her brother. In due course, the maid from the prior evening arrived with a tray of eggs, bacon, toast, porridge, and tea.

"Thank you, Maureen," Jessamine said.

The maid said nothing, but deposited the food on the table and picked up the tray. Jessamine's quick glance revealed the absence of a sugar bowl. "Excuse me, but have you any sugar for the tea?"

"I'm too busy to get it, but you're welcome to fetch it from the kitchen yourself."

Jessamine's brows lifted. First Carter had been rude, and now Maureen. Was the entire staff nasty, or were they being awful just to her? The woman had been mostly pleasant when Lady Amelie was there, so it was probably something personal. Nevertheless, Jessamine couldn't imagine what she'd done, unless it was simply general resentment at her station in life. *I'm not good enough to be accepted upstairs, nor low-born enough to be welcome below. I face snobbery on both sides.*

She ate quickly, drinking her tea without sugar. With time to spare until she was to meet Amelie at the stables, Jessamine returned to her room, sat at the desk, and began a letter to Mr. Abernathy. Although she didn't want the Fosters to know precisely where she'd gone, Jessamine had no objection to letting the attorney know her address. No sooner had she written the salutation, however, she paused. What reason should she give for having left Arbor Manor? To criticize the motives of a relative would be unseemly, so should she pretend her employment had been her own idea?

Dear Mr. Abernathy,

Due to a disagreeable arrangement with the Fosters, I've quit Arbor Manor and am now earning my living as a governess in Kent. If Uncle Thackery asks, you may tell him I've written to you, but please don't disclose the address.

Very Sincerely,

Jessamine Foster

After she re-read the letter, she crushed it into a ball and lobbed it into the cold fireplace. *I ought not bother writing to him at all. Mr. Abernathy works for my uncle now, so why should he care what becomes of me?* A cloud of self-pity began to descend, but she didn't indulge it for long. A walk in the fresh morning air was just the thing to clear her head, so she made her way outside and into the garden. *Perhaps I'll find the stables a little early and introduce myself to Trask. And if he isn't amiable, I'll befriend the horses!*

Amused, Dallas watched his sister eat her breakfast with speed that would rival that of a starving man. "Hungry?"

"I'm trying to finish quickly so I can give Mrs. Crandall instructions about the picnic. Everything must fit into our saddlebacks without getting crushed."

"I'd forgotten about your picnic. Well, it's a fine day for it."

Amelie snatched up one last piece of toast before springing to her feet. She deposited a bacon-scented smack on his cheek and then dashed from the dining room without a backward glance.

"I've been thrown over for the companion," he murmured.

As Dallas finished his own leisurely breakfast, movement in the garden outside the window caught his eye. A woman in a form-fitting riding habit was wandering through an rose-bush-lined pathway. *Miss Foster cuts an elegant figure.* As she bent to smell one of the dainty new blooms, Dallas studied her profile. *I don't know why I didn't see it before, but she's a stunning beauty.* Frowning, he turned away from the window and returned to his morning paper.

Laughing, Jessamine and Amelie raced their mares across a field of gently waving grass. Chunks of rain-moistened earth flew in the wake of their horses' hooves. A narrow ditch transected their path, and they took the jump across with ease. Jessamine's hair, already in a precarious state underneath her hat, came loose from its pins and flowed down her back. When Amelie reined in her horse, Jessamine followed suit.

"I haven't had this much fun in ages," Amelie said.

"Nor I. You've a fine seat, milady. It was all I could do to keep up."

Amelie gave Jessamine a sidelong glance. "You flatter me, but I'll take the compliment. Come on; I know the perfect place for our picnic."

The two rode until they reached a broad stream, hugging the bank until they came upon a large weeping willow. The field beyond was dotted with a profusion of wildflowers, and Jessamine gasped with the beauty of it.

"You are fortunate indeed to live in such a lovely place."

"I like to think of this as my outdoor study," Amelie said. "I come here to be alone and daydream."

"It's very serene. I'm honored you've shared it with me."

"Knight's Keep is beautiful this time of year, but my favorite day is Christmas. Dallas started a new tradition by inviting the village children and their families to the house for a big party. The youngsters receive toys and clothes, and their parents leave with big hampers stuffed with food. It's ever so much fun."

"How wonderful." Jessamine was taken aback. *Among his other virtues, Lord Kirkendale is uncommonly generous. I daresay Aunt Rachel would consider his actions a scandalous waste of money.*

Amelie and Jessamine dismounted, looped their horses' reins onto a bush next to the stream, and carried their saddle-bags underneath the tree. Jessamine unfurled a blanket, tossed her hat to one side, and pulled her tousled tresses forward.

"I'm afraid I'm rather useless when it comes to arranging my own hair," she said, shaking it free. "I suppose with a bit of practice I'll get it right."

When she began to braid her hair once more, Amelie stopped her. "Oh, don't! With your hair down about your shoulders like that, you look like a Botticelli painting."

"I should hope it's one in which the lady is wearing clothes."

Amelie's peals of laughter started a bird from its perch in the tree overhead. "You've a wicked sense of humor, Miss Foster."

"It balances out my wicked temper."

"You simply must allow me to put flowers in your hair."

"Go on, then. Pick some flowers while I lay out our feast."

FRESHLY LAID horse tracks made it easy for Dallas to follow his sister's path. Although the route was circuitous, he finally spied Amelie picking flowers in a distant field of bluebells. As he moved closer, he spied Miss Foster sitting underneath the weeping willow tree. Her long dark wavy hair was loose of its ordinary constraints, and it had been decorated with elegant bluebells, fuzzy purple knapweed, and cheerful white and yellow wild strawberry blooms. Any uneasiness or worry Miss Foster had exhibited previously had given way to a carefree and happy contentment, and the total effect was enchanting. He hesitated a moment, reluctant to disturb the beautiful tableau, but then his sister spotted him.

"Dallas!" Amelie shrieked. "What are you doing here!"

Miss Foster's eyes grew wide, and she scrambled to her feet. "Milord!" She began to tear flowers from her hair.

"Don't let me spoil your fun." Dallas removed his hat, plucked one of the bluebells from Amelie's hand, and stuck it behind his ear. "In fact, I'll join in."

"It's not quite the same somehow," Amelie said.

A whisper of a smile lit Miss Foster's face, but she didn't slow her efforts to make herself presentable. Dallas tied his horse next to the two mares.

"How did you find us?" Amelie demanded.

"The earth is so moist from the recent rain it was easy to follow your horses' tracks," he replied. "And I came all the way out here because Mrs. Crandall said you'd forgotten this hamper." Dallas untied the wicker basket from his saddle. "Amongst its other treasures is a jar of pickled peaches."

"That's perfectly silly," Amelie said. "You just wanted to come to the picnic."

"You've found me out, as always. I couldn't stay away."

Dallas knelt on the blanket and opened the hamper. Although Miss Foster helped him unpack it, she seemed reluctant to meet his gaze.

"I do like pickled peaches very much," she murmured.

"I was hoping you would."

They feasted on a selection of chopped roast beef, chicken, and ham sandwiches, deviled eggs, potato salad, pickled peaches, gingerbread, and cheeses. Amelie and Miss Foster had brought flasks of tea, and Dallas supplemented that with one of lemonade. He told some amusing stories about Amelie's past mischiefs, and she retaliated with stories about his own misadventures.

"And you, Miss Foster?" he asked. "Have you always been as perfectly behaved as you are at present?"

"I'm afraid my temper has frequently given me cause for regret."

"Who was the target of your ire, if I may ask?"

"My cousin and I don't get along at all. It was a shame, really, since my mother always wished we'd be friends."

"What's the worst quarrel you ever had with her?" Amelie asked, wide-eyed.

"You ought not be so personal," Dallas cautioned.

"It's all right. My cousin took something of mine that was very precious to me and damaged it deliberately." Miss Foster paused. "I-I gave her quite a smack in return."

"Oh, is that all?" Amelie said. "I've given Dallas a few smacks and he deserved every one of them."

His sister went off to chase butterflies while Miss Foster packed the remains of the picnic for the return trip. Dallas cleared his throat. "I'd like to offer my apologies for last night, Miss Foster. I was entirely unclear with my instructions, and I'm afraid I caused you unpardonable discomfort."

He'd meant the apology to remove any remnant of strain between them, but it seemed to have the opposite effect. Her expression cooled, and she lowered her lashes. "Please don't distress yourself any further, sir. Every household has different rules, and I should have asked the housekeeper about it." She stood. "If you'll excuse me, I'm going to pick some flowers for my room."

As she wandered into the field, Dallas frowned and shook his head slightly. *What am I doing, begging the pardon of a servant? Perhaps I should take my leave.* After he secured the hamper onto his saddle, Dallas untied his horse and mounted it.

"Amelie, I'm off," he called out.

His sister looked up at the sound of his voice and waved. Without sparing a glance for Miss Foster, Dallas turned his horse and cantered back the way he'd come.

CHAPTER 5
TELL-TALE HEARTS

Dallas handed off his horse to Trask, with instructions to a stableboy as to the hamper, and then loped up the stairs to his room. After ringing for his valet, he washed his face and hands, laughing when he discovered a bluebell was still stuck behind his ear.

Baum appeared in the doorway of the bathroom. "Would you like me to lay out your dinner clothes, sir?"

"Not yet. Draw me a bath, would you?" Dallas asked.

"Very good, sir."

The hot fragrant water proved relaxing, and Dallas found his thoughts wandering to the picnic under the weeping willow. Mrs. Crandall had packed all manner of good things to eat, and he'd enjoyed himself immensely. If he were to be truthful, however, the food was only a small part of it. The vision of Miss Foster with her unbound hair continued to burn in his mind's eye. He would have liked to arrange her hair around her shoulders before leaning in to steal a kiss or two from those tempting lips. Suddenly he came to his senses almost as sharply as if his valet had dropped a chamberpot full of ice water over his head. *I'm a dreadful scoundrel.*

A CHILLY WIND presaged the imminent arrival of a rainstorm, so Jessamine and Amelie left the site of their picnic and urged their horses back to Knight's Keep. Along the way, Jessamine tried to decide why Lord Kirkendale had attended their picnic. He'd worn a stylish tweed Norfolk jacket, white jodhpurs, and sleek black boots, so perhaps he meant to dazzle her with his appearance. *If that was his intent, I believe I acquitted myself admirably. I hope His Lordship understands his charms are wasted on me. He'd best go back to Miss Hightower.*

"After dinner tonight, let's meet in the library," Amelie said. "You can read aloud, if you're up to it."

"Just the two of us? I can't imagine a more pleasant evening," Jessamine replied.

"You know, I've been trying to work out why Dallas came to our picnic today," Amelie said. "I think he must have been worried I was going to tie you to a tree or some such trick."

Jessamine laughed. "And here I thought perhaps your brother was observing my abilities as a companion."

"Perhaps it was both," Amelie replied. "Or perhaps it was neither. I noticed how much he admired you with the flowers in your hair."

"His admiration was for your handiwork, I'm certain. You have an artistic bent, milady. In fact, I'd like to see you draw."

"A cat can draw better than I can. No, I'm convinced my brother was mesmerized by your beauty."

Dismayed, Jessamine gasped. "Lady Amelie, I implore you not to speak of such things. Since no respectable alliance is possible between His Lordship and I, such talk will damage my reputation. Surely you can see that? Whatever passed for admiration was merely politeness."

Amelie's blue eyes widened. "Oh, Miss Foster, I meant nothing by my remark whatsoever. Forgive me, please."

"No forgiveness is necessary, milady, but for my sake, let it be. A man may admire a woman, and vice versa, without any action being taken to further the relationship. Such is the nature of men and women."

"So you admire my brother?"

"I didn't say that!"

Amelie giggled. "I'm teasing you."

Jessamine sighed. "I think I'd much rather you tie me to the tree."

JUST BEFORE SEVEN O'CLOCK, Jessamine made her way to the schoolroom. Maureen arrived with her dinner tray shortly thereafter, placed the dishes on the table, and left without a word. The maid's continued chilly attitude was grating, and Jessamine was further annoyed she'd not been given any sugar for her tea yet again. *Maureen invited me to fetch it myself, and so I will!*

As Jessamine descended the servant's staircase, she could hear the staff conversing from inside their dining room on the lower level.

"I saw her prancing around the garden as bold as brass, right in front of His Lordship's breakfast room...no doubt trying to catch his eye."

"Miss Hightower will have something to say about that!"

"Have ye heard the way she talks? I expect she looks down her nose at us, that's fer certain."

"Shut it, the lot of you. Mr. Baum says Miss Foster is a

sweet, well-bred young lady who has had some bad luck. You're all being unkind just because she's such a good-looking girl."

That last voice belonged to Trask, whom Jessamine had met at the stables. *He, at least, is gracious enough to take up for me.* Slightly shaken, she continued on to the kitchen, where the harried cook was muttering to herself. When Jessamine cleared her throat, Mrs. Crandall looked up from her task of kneading dough. Her brows lifted.

"You must be the new companion everyone's talking of."

"Yes, ma'am. My name's Miss Foster and I came for some sugar," Jessamine said.

"I'm Mrs. Crandall and it's lovely to meet you. There are a half dozen sugar bowls on the shelf just over your shoulder. Help yourself."

"Thank you." Jessamine located a sugar bowl and turned to leave.

"Er...Miss Foster? Pay no attention to that lot in the next room. I can hear them gossip all the way in here, and it's all rubbish."

Jessamine gave her a grateful smile. "Thank you, Mrs. Crandall. I appreciate your kindness."

Trask is friendly and now Mrs. Crandall. Perhaps the good and the bad balance one another in the end.

THE PLEASANT TASTE of lemon tart lingered on Dallas's tongue as he watched Amelie lick the last bit of whipped cream from her fork.

"I'm meeting Miss Foster after dinner," Amelie said. "She's to read to me."

"I'll go with you," Dallas said. "I'd like to hear her read."

As he escorted his sister into the library, Miss Foster was waiting next to one of the bookshelves, perusing the titles. When she turned her large blue eyes in his direction, his palms grew moist and his mouth went dry. *Suddenly I'm unnerved by my sister's companion?*

"If it's Poe you're looking for, he's over here." He selected the book and handed it to her. "I hope you don't mind if I listen."

"Not at all, milord."

While Miss Foster turned to the beginning of the story, he poured himself a brandy. Although she demurred his offer of sherry, she accepted a glass of water. Amelie curled up on the sofa, but Dallas chose a wing chair directly across from Miss Foster. *So I can enjoy the view.*

JESSAMINE IGNORED Kirkendale as best she could and focused her energies instead on her reading. The occasional crack of thunder, steady thrum of rain against the library windows, and the cozy fire lent the room the perfect atmosphere for Edgar Allan Poe. She applied to the words all the passion and drama the story deserved, and her audience of two rewarded her by paying rapt attention. *The Tell-Tale Heart* was not overly long, but when Jessamine paused just after the old man in the story was murdered, sounds of protest ensued.

"Oh no, Miss Foster, you cannot stop there," Amelie exclaimed. "I can't bear it!"

"Nor I," Kirkendale added.

Jessamine stifled a smile. "Patience! I'm only halfway through."

After taking a sip of water, she resumed the story, which ended with the narrator's confession. Amelie gasped and sat back. "Was the heart truly beating then? Did the officers know all along?"

"No, the narrator was completely mad," Jessamine replied.

"I think he wanted to be discovered," Kirkendale said. "He wanted someone to know how clever he'd been."

"He was stupid! All he needed to do was to shut up and he would have gotten away with his crime," Amelie said.

"It's not always easy to hide your feelings, milady," Jessamine said. "Oftentimes the body betrays what the mind is thinking."

Recognition suddenly dawned on Amelie's face. "Oh, I think I understand. It's when a man and a woman like each other romantically, but they can't say so. They become flushed when they're in the same room, and their hands tremble, and they avoid looking at one another or sometimes they stare when they think nobody's looking."

Kirkendale peered at his sister. "How do you know all that?"

"I've seen it for myself recently."

To Jessamine's dismay, the book in her hand slipped to the floor, landing on the rug with a loud thump. "How clumsy," she murmured.

She and Kirkendale both reached for the book. When their fingers accidentally touched, she drew her hand back as if burned. "I'm so sorry."

"Forgive me," he said at the same time.

Amelie rolled her eyes and sighed. Whatever else she meant to say next was interrupted by a sneeze.

"Bless you," Jessamine said. "I hope you didn't catch a chill this afternoon."

"It was just a sneeze," Amelie said. "I'm perfectly fine."

"Nevertheless, let's get you to bed straightaway."

"I'll check on you in the morning," Kirkendale called out as Jessamine ushered his sister toward the door.

Jessamine helped Amelie undress, tugged a nightgown over her dark curls, and tucked her into bed. The storm was still raging outside, with loud cracks of thunder. Amelie shuddered and pulled the covers up to her chin. "Ooh, I'm too scared to sleep. Will you read to me a while?"

"I'll find something in the library. Close your eyes and I'll be right back."

The gaslights in the hallway and stairwell were turned low, but were adequate to light Jessamine's way as she found her way downstairs. The library was still dimly illuminated by the fire in the fireplace. As she moved toward one of the gaslights to turn the flame up higher, Lord Kirkendale peered out from his wing chair.

"Oh, hello," he said. "How's my sister?"

Startled, Jessamine blanched. "Pardon me, Your Lordship. I didn't mean to intrude on your privacy. Lady Amelie asked me to read to her, and I was hoping to find a fairy tale."

Kirkendale set down his snifter of brandy, beckoning her over as he stood.

"I have just the thing." He led her over to a wall of handsomely bound books and turned up the light in the nearest sconce. His fingertip traveled lightly over the spines of the books, until he found the one he sought. "Here we are. *Children's and Household Tales* by the Brothers Grimm."

As Kirkendale gave her the book, he was so close she could smell the slight hint of spirits on his breath. *Could I taste the brandy on his lips if we kissed?* She was glad the dim light hid the blush that was surely coloring her skin. "Thank you for the book. I'm sure your sister will enjoy it."

A muscle worked in Kirkendale's jaw, and he gave her a curt nod. *Have I annoyed him in some fashion?* Bewildered, Jessamine fled the library as quickly as decorum would allow.

Upon her return to Amelie's room, she discovered the girl had already fallen asleep despite the storm raging outside. Jessamine left *Children's and Household Tales* on the bedside table for another time, turned out the lights, and closed the door behind her.

As she prepared for bed, Lord Kirkendale's fragrance still lingered in her mind...along with a sense of shame. *I can't believe I had such a silly thought. Thank goodness the man can't read minds.*

IN THE EARLY MORNING FOG, Olivia rode Dresden toward a gnarled oak tree at the outskirts of Lord Kirkendale's estate. Maureen was waiting for her there, wrapped in a shawl. As Olivia dismounted, she gave the maid an annoyed glance. "Couldn't you have picked somewhere indoors? I hope this means you have information for me."

"Aye, Miss Hightower." From a pocket in her apron, Maureen withdrew a wrinkled letter. "I nicked this for you. The governess wrote it and then tossed it into the fireplace."

Olivia quickly read the contents. "Interesting. Does Lord Kirkendale show any particular interest in Miss Foster?"

"I'm not sure, but he's not blind. Although it pains me to say so, Miss Foster is the finest-looking woman I've ever seen."

Olivia's eyes narrowed. "Beauty is in the eye of the beholder. Do you know anything else about her?"

"Trask mentioned she's a gentleman's daughter whose estate was entailed away when her parents died."

"That gives me a bit to go on." Olivia tossed a gold coin at Maureen's feet before mounting her horse once more. "If there's anything else you think I should know, send word. There's more gold where that came from."

CHAPTER 6

PIED PIPER

Sir Bartholomew was pouring over a ledger in his study when Olivia tracked him down. "Do you have a moment, Papa?"

A crease appeared between his eyes as he looked up. "If you must."

She hastened inside. "You and Lord Kirkendale are great friends. Can't you find a way to announce our engagement?"

"We aren't great friends, in point of fact. We're neighbors and business associates, after a fashion. But at any rate, I've no doubt he'll marry you, sooner or later."

"The upcoming Season will be my seventh, and my friends are beginning to wonder if I'll be an old maid."

"You're female, and I'm certain you have tricks up your sleeve. Can't you induce Kirkendale to marry you on your own?"

"Papa!"

"Don't pretend to take offense. I've noticed the lad can't seem to keep a governess for his sister. Although I can't prove anything, I'm positive you've had a hand there."

"I make no apologies for protecting what is mine."

"I didn't ask for any, but you should take care he never finds out who engineered his difficulty."

"If you give him a deadline, it won't matter if he knows or not."

"Fine. I'll tell him the engagement must be announced by Christmas or pressure will be brought to bear."

Christmas! Papa can be so stupid sometimes. Olivia forced a tight smile. "Lady Amelie's first Season is coming up, and I daresay he'd like it to go smoothly."

"Meaning?"

"I'm not stupid, Papa. I know you've got some sort of leverage on him. Now is the perfect time to wield it."

"Your perspicacity is impressive. I'll see what I can do."

"In the meantime, I'm taking Mama to town on business."

Sir Bartholomew peered at his daughter. "I hope your business is with a modiste and with no one else?"

"Naturally."

Her father frowned. "I warn you not to meddle, Olivia. Leave it to me."

She was all smiles. "Of course, Papa."

DALLAS WAS READING a book in the library when his butler ushered a gentleman caller inside. The tall, slender newcomer had an arresting, impish face and a disarming smile.

"The Lord Fitzwilliam Stansbury," the butler announced.

With a warm smile on his face, Dallas strode over to give his friend a vigorous handshake and a slap on the back. "It's good to see you, Stansbury. To what do I owe the honor of your visit?"

"When I got to town, I discovered my staff was in the midst

of cleaning my Belgrave Square townhouse. So I decided to hop on a train and come here for a few days until the dust settles…if you don't mind. Besides which, I have yet to give Amelie her birthday present."

"You're always welcome. In fact, I'd like you to meet Amelie's new companion."

"Let me guess; she's a crone with a wart?"

"Quite the opposite, but Miss Foster does baffle me. I'd like your opinion, in fact."

"Of opinions, I have many, and I'm always willing to part with them free of charge. What seems to be the problem?"

"She's been here several weeks now, and although she and Amelie have become fast friends, every time I'm near her she turns to ice."

"Perhaps she'll thaw in my company. I've been told women melt in my presence."

"You have not."

"Well, no, I haven't. Not in so many words."

Dallas laughed. "Come, I'll introduce you. She's in the music room with Amelie."

CRISP NEW SHEET music from *The School Girl* rested on the grand piano's music rack, begging to be played. While Jessamine turned the pages, Amelie's fingers coaxed a spritely cheerful tune from the keyboard. After humming along for a few notes, Jessamine broke into full voice. When the song ended, she and Amelie were surprised to hear applause. They turned to discover Lord Kirkendale and another gentleman had entered the music room.

"That was marvelous," said the stranger.

"Stansbury!" Amelie jumped to her feet and ran to embrace him. "When did you get here?"

"Just now. I simply couldn't wait to see you."

"Yes, it's been far too long. One whole month, hasn't it been?"

"And each moment apart, a veritable torture." Over Amelie's head, Stansbury grinned and gave Jessamine a wink. "I saw *The School Girl* at the Prince of Wales Theatre in London not eighteen months ago. You two put that performance to shame."

Excessive praise, Jessamine knew, but it made her smile.

"Miss Foster, allow me to introduce the Lord Fitzwilliam Stansbury," Kirkendale said. "Stansbury, this is Miss Foster."

Jessamine extended her hand, and Stansbury grasped it with both of his.

"My dear Miss Foster, I pray you'll sing for me again," he said. "Perhaps we can have a musical evening while I'm here?"

"Yes, let's do," Amelie said. "I have sheet music from *A Gaiety Girl*."

"Perhaps you'd like to join us for dinner tonight, Miss Foster?" Kirkendale asked. "We can have an entertainment afterward."

"I'd be delighted," Jessamine said.

"Good. I look forward to it."

The Lord Fitzwilliam Stansbury let go of her hand, but the warmth of his skin lingered. Although the man was a trifle forward, Jessamine could not help but like him. His open and friendly nature brought a badly-needed buffer between her and Lord Kirkendale, in whose presence she could not relax. As the two men left the room, Jessamine noticed Lady Amelie watching her.

"You mustn't take Stansbury seriously. He's an awful flirt."

"Then we'll just be friendly acquaintances," Jessamine said. "Like your brother and I."

~

AFTER DALLAS RANG for a servant to show Stansbury to his room, he headed downstairs to the kitchen to confer with the cook regarding the extra dinner guests. His butler found him there a few minutes later.

"Sir Bartholomew Hightower has arrived just now, milord."

Although his first impulse was to send Hightower away, his concern for Gaston the colt led Dallas to the drawing room. His neighbor rose from the sofa as he appeared.

"Good afternoon, Sir Bartholomew. Is anything amiss with Gaston?" Dallas asked.

"Not at all. I've come on another matter entirely." He paused. "Your late father and I understood one another quite well over the years, and I've been gratified by my continued relationship with you."

Dallas's eyes narrowed slightly, but he said nothing.

"At any rate, I certainly hope nothing casts a shadow on Lady Amelie's upcoming Season," Sir Bartholomew continued.

"I can't imagine anything would, but I'm sure you're here to enlighten me."

"Lady Hightower and I would dearly love to announce your engagement to Olivia as soon as possible. I think Lady Amelie's debutante ball would provide the perfect occasion for a formal announcement."

"And if I prefer to wait?"

"Consequences will ensue."

His hands clenched at his sides, Dallas took a half-step

forward. He was gratified to see fear flicker across Sir Bartholomew's face.

"Good day to you, sir," Dallas said. "I'm sure you can find your way out."

He turned on his heel and strode from the drawing room. Amelie's future meant everything to him, and Bartholomew's veiled threat made him furious. Worse, he was impotent to retaliate or refuse the man's demands. Unseemly though it was to speak ill of the dead, he cursed his father for forcing him into this Faustian bargain. *The sins of the fathers are visited upon the children. Never more true than now.*

After changing into his riding clothes, he went to the stable. Against Trask's advice, Dallas selected Folderol to ride. *If I don't work some of this anger out, I'll be poor company at dinner.* As the horse streaked across a field, trying to dislodge his unwelcome rider, Dallas leaned into the wind. *I wish I could dislodge Sir Bart so easily.*

WHEN DRESSING THAT NIGHT, Jessamine chose one of her mother's dinner gowns. The full dove gray skirt emphasized her slim waist, and the graceful black bodice revealed the top of her shoulders and throat. She applied her hairbrush to her loose locks, resigned to twisting it into a low knot again. Amelie arrived at her room, clad in a dainty pink dress with white embroidery. To Jessamine's surprise, she had her lady's maid in tow.

"Oh, that's a pretty gown!" Amelie exclaimed. "I brought Edith to arrange your hair."

"How truly thoughtful of you, milady," Jessamine said. "And your gown is lovely too." Her eyes fell to an enameled locket hanging from a chain around Amelie's neck. "What a beautiful necklace!"

"Isn't it? It's a birthday gift from Stansbury. He's always so good to me."

Amelie sat on the bed to watch as Edith parted Jessamine's hair into sections and then rolled it into a sophisticated pompadour high on top of her head. The maid loosened a few wavy curls to drift across Jessamine's neck for a romantic look.

"Edith, that's gorgeous," Amelie said. "Now that I'm eighteen, I'd like you to do that with my hair sometime."

After thanking the maid profusely, Jessamine accompanied Amelie downstairs. As she approached the drawing room, Jessamine was struck by how much she was looking forward to the evening. The last time she'd had any fun was before her parents died. Amelie threaded her arm through Jessamine's. "I'm so glad you're here."

"So am I," Jessamine.

Lord Kirkendale and Lord Stansbury were warming themselves next to the fire when Jessamine and Amelie entered the room.

"Here we are," Amelie announced.

"Good evening," Jessamine said.

As the gentlemen gazed at her, she felt a subtle shift in the room's atmosphere. She'd entered Knight's Keep as a servant and would leave as one, but for tonight she was a cultivated young gentlewoman in a pretty dress amongst friends. Renewed confidence coaxed her charm to the surface, and she gave the earl and his guest a dazzling smile. Although she couldn't be certain, she thought she heard Lord Stansbury murmur, "My word," under his breath before he and the earl both sketched a bow.

OVER DINNER, Dallas found Miss Foster to be beautiful, vivacious, and intelligent. *What a change has been wrought in her from the first time we met!* His eyes slid to Stansbury, who was roaring with laughter over Miss Foster's last witty remark. *So Stansbury has brought out Miss Foster's warmer side after all.* Dallas reached for his wine and drank deeply to blunt the sting of the realization. *Surely I'm not jealous my closest friend has had more success with the lady than I have?* He drained his glass and gestured to the footman to refill it. *Since I'm forced to marry Olivia, my feelings don't matter in any case. Let Stansbury enjoy his flirtation. Someone, at least, should be happy.*

Before the footman could pour the wine, the stem of Dallas's wine glass snapped in two under the pressure of his grip, slicing the pad of his thumb in the process. "Blazes," he muttered.

Amelie, Stansbury, and Miss Foster all gasped as blood welled up in the cut and ran down into his palm. He quickly wrapped his thumb in a handkerchief and excused himself to tend to his wound.

As his valet helped him dress his wound with a gauzy bandage, a question popped into his mind. "Baum, do you think a man should sacrifice his own happiness for someone he loves?"

The valet pondered the issue a moment. "Most people would believe such conduct to be noble."

Dallas chuckled. "Very diplomatic reply, but I asked what *you* thought."

"I think a very clever man would find a way to secure his happiness and protect his loved one at the same time."

"Do you now?"

Although Baum's response surprised Dallas, it also lifted his mood. If only he could navigate through his present diffi-culty with Sir Bartholomew, what a pleasure it would be to contemplate life with a woman like Miss Foster! *Perhaps if I set my mind to it, anything is possible.* A certain devil-may-care attitude came over him at the thought he could reshape his destiny.

A few minutes later he rejoined Stansbury, Amelie, and Miss Foster in the dining room for dessert. Three pairs of eyes regarded him with concern.

"Are you all right?" Amelie asked.

"Perfectly so." To prove it, Dallas stuck his gauze-wrapped thumb in the air. "It would take more than a cut to keep me from such pleasant company."

He gave Miss Foster a wink and his most wicked smile, and was rewarded by a blush.

LORD KIRKENDALE's change of demeanor sent a shockwave through Jessamine, from her head to her toes. *It's as if he knows what I look like in my chemise!* Since before dinner, the young earl had seemed distracted and saddened somehow, but now he was playful and bright. She wasn't the only one who'd noticed; Lord Stansbury also had a faint expression of puzzlement on his face. On the other hand, Amelie was too busy eating cake to pay much attention. Perhaps an excess of drink was responsible for his sudden warmth and for the broken glass...although he'd appeared perfectly sober beforehand. When he offered Jessamine his arm to escort her into the music room, Amelie exchanged a glance with Lord Stansbury.

As pleasurable as Lord Kirkendale's attentions were, Jessamine didn't know how to react. To assume an icy demeanor would be rude, but on the other hand she didn't want to encourage a relationship that would surely end in her leaving Knight's Keep without a reference. She settled on a course of polite reserve, although her gaze rested far too often on her employer to be perfectly correct. Her resolve nearly unraveled, however, when Amelie coaxed her brother into singing while she accompanied him. Kirkendale's clear tenor voice sent pleasurable shivers down her spine. If she weren't so mesmerized by his handsome face, she would have closed her eyes to enjoy the sensations he aroused.

When the earl finished his song, the mesmerizing effect his voice had on Jessamine lifted. As she and Lord Stansbury applauded, she had a sudden realization. *I thought I could avoid falling in love and already I feel as if I'm under his thrall. Is the Earl of Kirkendale a Pied Piper of young women or am I just weak-willed?*

For the duration of the evening, Jessamine challenged herself not to give Lord Kirkendale more than a glance. *If I simply behave normally, nobody has to know the strength of my attraction. Few women would not be drawn to the man, but I needn't assume my feelings are anything more than physical. I'm not a ninny!* The more she attempted to ignore him, however, the more determined he seemed to catch her eye. Finally, he asked Amelie to play a waltz. As the first few notes poured from the piano, Kirkendale extended his hand to Jessamine.

"Miss Foster, may I have this dance?"

FOR A FEW EXCRUCIATING MOMENTS, Dallas thought Miss Foster would demur. To his sweet relief, she rose and allowed him to lead her to the empty space between the piano and the seating area. As they began to move to the music, it took a few steps for them to find their rhythm. Her color rose. "I'm sorry," she murmured. "I'm dreadfully out of practice."

"I'm glad."

Confused, she scrunched up her nose in such an adorable manner he had to stifle the impulse to kiss it. "Whatever do you mean?"

"Only that perfect people are extremely dull. Also, your lack of practice makes me feel very superior indeed. All in all, I'd say your response is politic and has my approval."

Miss Foster laughed, tossing a glance over one shoulder toward Amelie. "Your brother is quite charming."

Amelie giggled. "Indeed he can be charming, when he's not being bossy."

When the song ended, Dallas reluctantly relinquished Miss Foster to Stansbury for another waltz. Afterward she turned the pages for Amelie as she played Mozart. He and Stansbury lurked in the back of the room with snifters of brandy.

"You wanted my opinion on the companion before," Stansbury said, low. "Do you still?"

"I suppose so, although I warn you if it differs significantly from mine I'll turn you out of the house."

"Miss Foster is perfectly wonderful and I think you should marry her—if she'll have you, of course."

Dallas lifted his eyebrows. "She's penniless, and almost completely without family."

"Families can be complicated and annoying, and you've got enough money for the both of you. Besides which, it's too late. You're smitten."

"Nonsense. You're overstating the situation."

"Admit it. I've never seen you act this way before."

"I've only known Miss Foster for a little while. And I confess, my impression is that you're keen on her yourself."

"Indeed I would be...but I've already formed an attachment to someone else."

"Really?" Dallas exclaimed. "Do I know the lady?"

He winced. "Yes, but I'd rather not confess it yet. I'm not

completely certain of her feelings, you see, and I've not spoken with her guardian. But as soon as I'm assured my regard is returned, you'll be the first to know."

"Then we both have our work cut out for us. Sir Bart paid me a visit today. He insists on making a formal announcement of my engagement to Olivia in a month."

"No! That's awfully overbearing of him."

"On his deathbed, my father made me promise to continue his business relationship with Sir Bart by selling him my best horses on extremely favorable terms. I've often wondered if blackmail wasn't involved."

"You've never been specific about it, but I guessed something was amiss there."

"My father also told me my marriage to Olivia was arranged. I'd resigned myself to it until very recently."

Stansbury's gaze fell on Miss Foster. "I can't imagine who might have changed your mind," he said drily.

"I must learn what the blackmail was about and put an end to it."

"Do you have any ideas?"

"When I get to London I'll visit my solicitor. He handled my father's affairs and may be able to bring some light to bear on the situation."

"Let me know if there's anything I can do to help. Bart is a social-climbing, pretentious little twit." The reply was laced with venom.

"I'm touched by your loyalty," Dallas said.

Stansbury lifted his glass in a toast. "Cheers."

"Cheers."

CHAPTER 7

THE PARIS LILLY

Clad in an impeccably tailored suit, the private investigator ushered his client into his office and swept his hand toward the rose-patterned chair with red fringe. "Please be seated, Miss Hightower."

She settled herself and regarded the compact man with a gleam in her eye. "I hope you have something for me, Mr. Rivers."

"I've never failed you before, and this time is no different." He opened the file in front of him and skimmed its contents. "We may safely assume the letter you brought me was intended for Mr. Abernathy, the London attorney who manages the legal affairs of the Fosters. Miss Jessamine Foster's estate was entailed away from her and is now owned by Mr. Thackery Foster, her uncle."

"I know that already."

Mr. Rivers gave her a benevolent smile before he continued. "The girl has no money, dowry, or assets of any kind, nor could I find any scandal regarding Jesse or Minerva Foster, her deceased parents."

Olivia slumped in her chair and pouted. "That's too bad."

"But you'll be interested to know Jessamine Foster is related to the infamous Miss Lillian Perrisham, otherwise known as the Paris Lilly to her, um, sponsors."

A gasp of delight. "The courtesan? Oh, that's too droll. How closely are they related?"

"Miss Perrisham is the late Minerva Foster's aunt, although they were only a year apart in age."

"I couldn't be more pleased," Olivia said. "I can definitely do something with this information."

"A word of advice, Miss Hightower. Tread carefully where the Paris Lilly is concerned. She may be of the demimonde, but she's powerfully connected nevertheless."

"Don't be silly. I don't plan to blackmail her, do I?" Olivia retorted.

"I should hope not." Mr. Rivers slid the file across the desk to Olivia. "Shall I send my bill to your father?"

Olivia pulled a wad of paper money from her reticule. "I'll settle it now. No need to inform him of this matter at all."

CARTER HASTENED into the library with a silver salver in hand, interrupting a lively afternoon game of cards. Jessamine could not help but notice the footman's sour expression when he looked at her.

"I beg your pardon, but a message for the Lord Fitzwilliam Stansbury has arrived just now."

"Thank you." Stansbury glanced at the envelope. "Ah, it's from my butler."

While Stansbury was reading his letter, Amelie showed her hand. "Ha! I win!"

"You little minx." Kirkendale gathered up the cards and began to shuffle.

Stansbury frowned. "My townhouse is ready."

"You don't seem very happy about it," Kirkendale said.

"It's just that I've been having such a good time these last few days at Knight's Keep, I don't want to leave." He brightened. "Why don't the three of you come to London with me? The Season has not yet begun in earnest, but there are still plenty of diverting activities to keep us amused."

"Oh, yes! Send some of the staff on ahead to open our townhouse, Dallas," Amelie urged.

"Actually, I already have," Kirkendale replied. "Can you ladies can be ready to leave the day after tomorrow?"

Jessamine and Amelie exchanged a delighted glance.

"I'd say it's entirely possible, wouldn't you, milady?" Jessamine said.

Amelie jumped to her feet. "I must speak with Edith!"

As Jessamine packed for the journey to London, she hummed a cheerful tune. *Perhaps I won't have a Season, but living vicariously through Lady Amelie is the next best thing.* Because she'd gone shopping with her mother so frequently as a child, Jessamine knew where to find the best milliners and modistes on Amelie's behalf. She'd come to regard the girl almost like a younger sister and was looking forward to her triumphs with eager anticipation. In addition, she would accompany Amelie whenever she needed a chaperone, such as visits to museums or horseback riding in the park. *Things are not all bad!*

Since the night when Lord Kirkendale cut his thumb, Jessamine had been slightly wary of his intentions. He'd been extremely gentlemanly in his behavior, however, giving no cause for alarm. She'd been included in every meal and entertainment thereafter, and despite her earlier resolve, she felt her guarded manner toward him slipping. *Even though I mustn't reveal my feelings, it's wonderful to be in his company.* In addition, after several years in the Fosters' dour presence, she soaked up her present congenial atmosphere like a morning glory blossom reaching for dawn.

As she arranged her gowns in her trunk, she caught sight of her mother's debutante dress. She lifted it out, admiring Hannah's clever handiwork in repairing the garment. The maid had actually replaced both sleeves with a gossamer fabric reclaimed from another one of her mother's old dresses. The beautiful white gown looked even better than before in Jessamine's opinion, and she held the garment up to the full-length mirror to admire her reflection. *I'm so glad I saved the dress from Charlotte, but it's a shame it will never be worn.*

Amelie entered the room and appeared in the mirror behind her. Her mouth formed a small O. "That dress is exquisite!"

"It was the gown my mother wore when she was presented to the queen years ago." Jessamine hesitated briefly before holding it out. "Would you like to try it on?"

"Could I? I'll be ever so careful!"

After Jessamine helped her into the dress, Amelie drank in her reflection, turning this way and that. "I feel like a princess. I've never worn such a pretty dress before."

A lump formed in Jessamine's throat. "You may have it, if you like. It would work for your presentation or for a ball. The train can be gathered up in the back into a bustle."

"Miss Foster...may I call you Jessamine? You're an angel." Amelie stood on her tiptoes to kiss Jessamine's cheek. "I'm not sure I could ever be as generous as you."

"It's not hard to be generous when you care about someone, milady. And anyway, just before you came in I was wishing someone would wear the dress at least once more." *If it can't be me, I want it to be Lady Amelie.* Jessamine surreptitiously wiped away the moisture spilling down her cheek. "Shall we show your brother and Lord Stansbury?"

"Oh, yes...and please call me Amelie!"

THE HEAVILY VEILED hat Olivia wore as she made an afternoon call to a certain Piccadilly address might not have been au courant, but fashion was the last thing on her mind. As she waited for Miss Perrisham to join her in the drawing room, she could not help but admire the exquisite, tasteful furniture, oriental rugs, crystal chandeliers, and expensive paintings rendered by the best known artists of the age. Olivia had been surprised when the liveried butler showed her into the sophisticated drawing room, having imagined the house to be swathed in red carpets and drapes, and the artwork to reflect the basest of human instincts. A fabulously jeweled Fabergé egg caught her eye from its perch on an étagère. *Apparently being a courtesan pays well.*

Indeed, when the lady of the house appeared, she was not dripping with heavy diamond jewelry, or clad in a low-cut gown, nor was her face painted in garish colors. In her late thirties, Miss Perrisham was past the freshest bloom of youth, but she was astonishingly beautiful nonetheless. Her hair and attire was indistinguishable from that of the most elite women Olivia had ever seen, and her carriage was almost regal. Her strong eyebrows framed large, heavily lashed blue eyes, her features were even, and her figure would make any man's head turn. Furthermore, the family resemblance to Jessamine Foster was obvious. A pang of jealousy shot through Olivia, until she reminded herself of the mission at hand.

Miss Perrisham tilted her head to one side. "I'm sorry...Miss Bones was it? Would you be so kind as to remove your hat? I feel as if I'm talking to a beekeeper."

Olivia felt her face warm, but she unpinned the hat and set it down next to her on the sofa. Miss Perrisham settled herself in a chair and folded her hands on her lap.

"Are we acquainted, Miss Bones?"

"I'm acquainted with your great-niece, Miss Jessamine Foster." Other than a slight lifting of one eyebrow, Olivia saw no sign of recognition on the woman's handsome visage. Nevertheless, she was not dissuaded. "I just thought you should know Miss Foster has been forced for financial reasons to work for Lord Kirkendale, as a companion to his sister."

"What is your interest in the matter?"

"His Lordship is a business associate of my father. I met poor Miss Foster at his estate in Kent, and she seemed desperately unhappy."

"I see."

"I feel awful that she's been reduced to circumstances which are little better than a servant. If she were my relative, I'd be compelled to intervene."

Miss Perrisham gave her a serene smile as she rose, signaling the end to Olivia's visit.

"Thank you so much for calling on me, Miss Bones." She rang for a footman. "William will show you out."

Olivia jammed her hat on her hair and fled. The Paris Lilly had turned out to be more intimidating than she had anticipated. In the carriage on the way back to Pimlico, she was dismayed to discover a copious amount of perspiration had soaked through her dress underneath her arms, leaving dark semi-circles in the light gray wool. Had the elegant Miss Perrisham noticed? She took a deep breath and tried to relax. Why should she be cowed by a woman of ill repute and low morals? Besides which, her plan was very clever and she'd executed it beautifully. *My visit will prompt Miss Perrisham to involve herself in Miss Foster's life, thus tainting the girl for polite Society forever. Dallas will want nothing to do with the great-niece of an infamous courtesan. I'll fit into his life quite nicely after that.*

As soon as her visitor left, Lillian intercepted her footman and thrust money into his hands. "Take a taxi and follow that girl's carriage. I want to know who she is."

William darted out the door, and Lillian moved to the window to make sure her footman was successful in hailing a hansom cab before the girl's carriage drove off. *If her name is actually Miss Bones, mine is Lady Randolph!* She returned to the drawing room and poured herself a glass of sherry. Although she'd perfected the art of maintaining a serene countenance, she was actually in an emotional tailspin. *How did the young chit discover my connection with Jessamine after I've taken such pains to hide it?* Furthermore, if the girl's allegations regarding Jessamine's dire financial circumstances were even partially true, Lillian would be furious. Of course, only a simpleton would believe "Miss Bones" truly had Jessamine's best interests at heart. *No doubt she is trying to ruin Jessamine socially by connecting her with me. I'd wager the girl has designs on the Seventh Earl of Kirkendale.*

INSIDE A PRIVATE TRAIN COMPARTMENT, Jessamine and Amelie made lists of what they would need to purchase for Amelie's Season. In the facing seats, Lord Kirkendale and Lord Stansbury debated whether or not motor cars would ever replace horse-drawn carriages.

"I took a ride in a Daimler Tonneau once," Stansbury said finally. "It was great fun at first, but when we got really going, I swallowed a bug. It rather put me off the whole concept of motor cars."

Clapping her hand over her mouth, Amelie convulsed with unladylike laughter. Stansbury pretended pique until Jessamine and Kirkendale chuckled, and then a grin spread over his face.

"I suppose next time I'll breathe through my nose."

After the merriment died down, Kirkendale peered at Amelie's notes. "I see you have your shopping plans in order."

"Yes, indeed." She slid her brother and Stansbury a mischievous glance. "And how do you two intend to occupy yourselves while we shop?"

"I plan to stay out of the way," Kirkendale replied.

"Wise course of action," Stansbury said. "You and I should make the rounds of the clubs to see who's in town."

Jessamine fervently hoped the Fosters had not yet arrived. Although London was a huge place, the Upper Ten frequented the same shops, restaurants, and venues. Would Mrs. Foster and Charlotte cut her if they happened to pass by on Bond Street, or would they take the time to sneer openly at her reduced circumstance? She guessed they would pretend not to see her, thereby disavowing any acquaintance. *Perhaps that's best so I don't have to introduce them to Amelie.*

"Where is your London house, Your Grace?" she asked.

"Eaton Square," Kirkendale replied.

"Dallas bought the townhouse last year, after *Maman*

died," Amelie said. "There were too many memories at the house in Mayfair, and neither one of us wanted to go back."

Jessamine smiled and nodded, but inwardly she sighed. The chance that she would encounter her relatives had just increased exponentially. *I suppose I will take what comes and deal with it accordingly.*

As the train pulled into Victoria Station, Stansbury nodded to Jessamine, kissed a giggling Amelie on the hand, and gave Kirkendale a firm handshake. "I suppose this is good-bye for now. Ring me up when you've settled in, Kirkendale, and we'll make plans."

"You finally installed a telephone?"

"I did, but I have to get the butler to show me how to use it. I find it rather intimidating."

"You do not," Kirkendale replied.

"Perhaps not, but you'll have the ladies believing not a word I say."

"I already don't believe a word you say," Amelie said. "But I do believe in *you*, Stansbury."

A flush spread from Stansbury's collar to his hairline. "That's quite lovely of you, Amelie."

Just as she finished lunch, Lillian's footman returned. "I followed the carriage to a townhouse in Pimlico. The girl's name is Miss Olivia Hightower, the daughter of Sir Bartholomew Hightower of Kent. Miss Hightower and her mother have been in residence for two days."

"Well done, William."

He produced a wad of pound notes and coins from his pocket. "Where would you like your change, Miss Perrisham?"

"You keep it. And tell Blaise to have the carriage ready to take me to the train station tomorrow morning."

"Right away, and thank you."

As Lillian sipped her tea, she weighed her options. *A little personal involvement is unavoidable at this point, but I'll take care to minimize the damage.*

CHAPTER 8
CONFIDENCES

Many of the servants from Knight's Keep had preceded their employer to London, so the Eaton Square townhouse was fully staffed when Lord Kirkendale and his party arrived. The only drawback for Jessamine was its location a half block away from the Fosters. *I suppose I should be grateful we are not next-door neighbors!*

"I've visited this house before, when my parents and I were in residence on Eaton Square," Jessamine said at tea. "It was owned by Lord Mordecai Plough back then."

"Your uncle inherited your father's townhouse, didn't he? Does that mean your relatives are in town?" Kirkendale asked.

"If they haven't yet arrived, it's certain they will shortly. My cousin Charlotte is making her debut this Season."

"Dallas and I will call on them when they are here, if you like," Amelie said.

"Of course. It would be a pleasure," Kirkendale said.

Jessamine struggled to formulated a response. "You're very kind, but don't call on the Fosters on my account. Our parting was awkward, and they would take no pleasure in seeing me again."

"But the Fosters are your only family!" Amelie exclaimed.

"That's true." Although Lillian Perrisham's name flashed into Jessamine's mind, she had no wish to bring her up. "But I didn't get along with my aunt or cousin, you see."

"Let me see if I have this straight," Kirkendale said. "Your uncle was your father's sole heir of a property in Derbyshire and a London residence, your cousin is making her debut, and you were turned out of the house to work for a living? I take it back; I have no wish to make the acquaintance of a man who could treat his own niece in such an infamous manner."

Her skin prickled with humiliation. "Please don't give it another thought."

"Dallas, you're embarrassing Jessamine," Amelie murmured.

"I don't mean to, but I must speak plainly." His eyes sought hers. "You should have your share of Society the same as your cousin."

The conversation had taken a more serious turn than Jessamine had intended, and she tried to change the subject. "If wishes were horses, beggars would ride. Besides which, I count myself extremely fortunate in my situation. I'm in London, and tomorrow Amelie and I shall go shopping together. I couldn't ask for anything better."

"Nor could I," Amelie said. "I must admit, however, the house seems empty without Stansbury. Should he ever marry, we won't see him at all. Dallas, do you know if he's looking for a wife?"

"He's been somewhat coy on the subject, but I understand he has his eye on a young lady," Kirkendale replied.

"Oh, no!" Amelie exclaimed.

Her brother gave her a quizzical look. "Don't you want the chap to be happy?"

She took a sip of water before making a reply. "Of course, but I-I dislike change."

"Perhaps the lady in question will be very amiable, and will add to your circle of friends," Jessamine said.

Amelie averted her eyes. "I'll reserve judgment until I meet her."

"That's the spirit," Lord Kirkendale said.

LILLIAN CAUGHT the morning train bound for Derbyshire. When she finally arrived at Arbor Manor, the butler hesitated to let her in. "I'm afraid the Fosters are not at home to visitors at the moment. They are preparing to depart for town."

In the entrance hall behind him, she could see sheets had been spread over some of the furniture. Nevertheless, she hadn't come all this way to be put off.

"Mr. Hattley, I insist you inform Mr. Foster that Miss Jessamine Foster's great-aunt is here to speak with him."

The butler peered at Lillian, recognition dawning on his lined face. "Miss Perrisham? Please come in." He ushered her into the drawing room. "I'll fetch Mr. Foster."

While she was alone, Lillian glanced around the room in dismay. It had been many years since she'd been to Arbor Manor, but she could find nothing to remind her of Minerva. The formerly tasteful drapes had been replaced with ostentatious and flounced window treatments which overpowered the architecture, and an explosion of feminine cushions populated every sofa and chair. It seemed to Lillian that the newest lady of the house had redecorated the room to impress, but had failed miserably.

A portly man hastened into the room just then, a worried expression on his ruddy face. "I'm Mr. Foster. Have you bad tidings regarding Jessamine?"

His concern appeared to be genuine, but Lillian was unimpressed. "Sir, I have been informed my niece is working as a companion, despite the fact I've been sending her sixty pounds per month since her parents passed away. That's in addition to generous birthday and Christmas gifts the past three years in the amount of one hundred pounds."

The gentleman stared at her as if she'd suddenly sprouted an extra head. "That's absurd."

"Is it?"

"I'm afraid there's been some mistake. If you'd been corresponding with Jessamine, I would know it. The post is placed on my desk daily."

"Who is in charge of the post?"

"The footman, Eugene."

"Summon him, please. And if Jessamine had a lady's maid I would like to speak with her as well."

At that, Mr. Foster puffed up. "I won't allow you to interrogate my staff, madame. I don't even know who you are, and I didn't think Jessamine had any other relatives."

Anger boiled up inside Lillian and spilled over. "Either I interrogate your staff or I'll involve the constable. I don't much like being stolen from, and I like mistreatment of my niece far less. The reason I have not been more personally involved in Jessamine's life is because she's Society and I'm demimonde. In my circles, I'm known as the Paris Lilly."

His ruddy complexion reddened further, and he was compelled to loosen his collar.

"You recognize my name, then. I expect you're wondering if I know about your peccadilloes," she continued. "Indeed, I do. Since your inheritance, you've kept a mistress in London, and

I've heard that your tastes in the bedroom are somewhat unique. Perhaps Mrs. Foster would enjoy a detailed description?"

White splotches appeared amongst the field of red. "That won't be necessary."

Mr. Foster summoned Eugene to the drawing room. The young man glanced from Lillian and back to his employer, as if perplexed. "Can I help you with something, sir?"

"Did you remember seeing any letters addressed to Miss Jessamine over the last two years?" Mr. Foster asked.

"Yes, sir. She corresponded with a gentleman in Kent a few times before she left."

"Nothing else?"

"N-No." The footman shrugged and shifted his weight. "I always bring the post to you, Mr. Foster. I don't really look at it."

Lillian gave him a sharp glance. "Then how did you know Miss Jessamine was corresponding with a gentleman in Kent?"

Eugene blanched and hung his head. "I might have looked at it a time or two."

"Eugene, it seems as if you have something you're not telling me," Mr. Foster said. "You haven't been nicking her letters, have you?"

The footman's head snapped up. "No, sir! Any letters that came for Miss Jessamine without a return address, I gave to Mrs. Foster like she asked."

Mr. Foster peered at him. "What are you talking about?"

"Miss Jessamine had an unwelcome admirer. The bloke is persistent, I must say. If I hadn't heard back from a girl after dozens of letters, I'd have given up."

"How frequently would you say these letters arrived?" Lillian asked.

"Every month. Sometimes more often."

"Did you happen to see what the letters contained?" Mr. Foster asked.

"No, sir." He gulped. "I'm not in trouble, am I?"

"Not at the moment," Mr. Foster said. "You may send in Hannah now."

After Eugene left, Lillian stood. "I would like to speak with Hannah in private. Is there somewhere the two of us could talk?"

Mrs. Foster stormed into the drawing room. "What on Earth is going on, Mr. Foster? We're going to miss our train." She glared at Lillian.

Hannah appeared in the doorway. "You wish to see me, sir?"

"Yes, Hannah," he replied. "Miss Perrisham wishes to have a word with you. Could you take her into the dining room?"

At the mention of Lillian's name, Mrs. Foster's glare changed into an expression of panic and her lips compressed into a thin line. She turned to leave, but her husband cut her off.

"Mrs. Foster, you will remain here," Mr. Foster said. "We need to have a little chat."

Since servants were busy preparing for the family's departure to town, Charlotte escaped the hullabaloo by sneaking up to the third floor. It always gave her a great deal of pleasure combing through whatever possessions her cousin had left behind in her former bedroom. While she was poking through a box of letters and mementos, she was startled to hear a conversation between Hannah and a strange woman. Their voices were coming through the vent, almost as clearly as if the speakers were in the room. When she heard Jessamine's name,

Charlotte dropped what she was doing and sprawled on the bed to listen. Hannah was describing in vivid detail what Jessamine's life had been like the past three years.

"And what little money Mr. Foster gave Miss Jessamine for Christmas, I think she used to pay her own ticket to Kent," she concluded. "I miss her something terrible, but I know she's better off away from here."

"Thank you for being a good friend to my great-niece."

Charlotte gasped. *Jessamine has a relative?*

"Your great-niece?" Hannah echoed. "Maybe Miss Jessamine could live with you, Miss Perrisham, and I could work for her again."

"Although I would wish otherwise, she cannot live with me and remain respectable. I don't wish to shock you, but I'm demimonde. My involvement in Jessamine's life must be kept in the strictest confidence."

Charlotte rolled over on her back and kicked her feet in the air with delight. *Jessamine's great-aunt is demimonde? I'll make sure everyone knows so she'll be ruined forever...but will anyone take my word for it? Too bad I don't have more concrete evidence.* She sat up straight when she remembered the box of keepsakes she'd found. *Didn't I see some letters addressed to Aunt Minerva from a Lillian Perrisham? If I read them, maybe I'll find some sort of proof.*

DALLAS PEERED AT HIS SOLICITOR, dumbfounded. "While he was working at the British embassy in Paris, my father kept a mistress? As vulgar as the situation may have been, I cannot believe he allowed himself to be blackmailed over something so trifling."

"I was under the strictest orders not to say anything to you until after your mother died," Mr. Oatley replied.

"Bartholomew Hightower worked as an embassy clerk at the same time as your father did, and so had firsthand knowledge of the affair."

"Sir Bart had not yet been elevated to the knighthood then."

"Your father assisted him with that in order to secure the man's silence."

Far from being upset, Dallas felt as if a great weight had been lifted from his shoulders. His short laugh was greeted by the solicitor's puzzled silence.

"Pardon me for my levity, Mr. Oatley, but I feel as if I should celebrate. Going forward, I needn't behave as if Sir Bart has any hold over me whatsoever. The need for secrecy is past, and I can't tell you what a relief it is."

"That's not the whole of it, I'm afraid. The illicit affair between your father and his mistress resulted in a child...a girl."

"What? Are you saying Amelie and I have a half-sister?"

"No, *you* have a half-sister. Lady Amelie is the child."

If he had not already been sitting down, Dallas's knees would have given way.

Throughout dinner, Amelie kept stealing glances at her brother's empty place at the table. "I can't believe Dallas threw us over to dine at his club."

Although Jessamine was no less disappointed, she kept it to herself. "At least he gave you the courtesy of a telephone call."

"I wanted to tell him about all the shops we visited, the fashionable ladies we saw, and the tea shop where we had lunch. I've never purchased so many wonderful things before!"

"I'm sure you can speak with him tomorrow. I'm glad we ordered your ball gowns first because they will take up most of the modiste's time, but we're not done shopping yet. We've daytime and dinner gowns to acquire along with all the accessories. You should also consider a new riding habit. Lord Kirkendale has given you a generous allowance, so you may as well use it."

A slender hand rose from Amelie's lap to cover her yawn. "Oh dear, but I'm tired! How am I ever to stay awake for a ball?"

"You won't have any problems with that. You'll be far too excited to fall asleep!"

"I'm afraid I'll have to turn in early tonight. I hope you won't be offended?"

"Not at all. The library is full of books, and I'm certain I shall pass the evening tolerably well."

True to her word, Amelie retired after eating her dessert, and Jessamine explored the library. She selected *The Time Machine* by H.G. Wells, threw a log on the fire, sat nearby with the book in her lap. Soon she became wholly absorbed in the narrative and didn't notice the hour growing quite late. Just as the clock struck midnight, she turned the last page. With a satisfied smile, she stood, stretched, and replaced the book on the shelf. Although she was not tired, she decided to go to bed anyway. *Otherwise I'll be no good to Amelie in the morning!*

As she dimmed the lights, movement by the door startled her. Lord Kirkendale was gripping the doorjamb, staring at her as if she were a ghost.

"I didn't hear you come in. Is everything all right?" she asked.

Kirkendale removed his hat and sketched a clumsy bow. As he straightened, his blond hair fell over his forehead and she could see his ascot tie was in disarray.

"Is it really you, or am I la-hucinating?" He tried to enunciate each syllable, but his tongue seemed to get the better of him.

Her eyes widened. *The man is in his cups!* "I'm not a hallucination, but I think perhaps you ought to retire."

Ignoring Jessamine's suggestion, he made his way carefully across the carpet until he was within arm's length of her. A cloud of gin vapors and other spirits enveloped her, and she stepped back. "Let me pour you some water, Your Lordship."

"You're a Seaven-hent angel."

As she went to the sideboard to get Kirkendale's water, he lowered himself into a chair. When she returned, he couldn't grip the glass with any certainty.

"Here, I'll hold it for you," she murmured.

He sipped the water, but quite a bit dribbled down his chin. Jessamine used her handkerchief to blot his face dry, and he caught her wrist. "I wish I hadn't met you."

A stab of pain at his words made her catch her breath. "I'm sorry you feel that way."

"No, you don't understand." He took the glass, drained it, and set it down on the floor. "I've been drinking an awful lot, so I know you won't remember any of this tomorrow. I have to marry Miss Tighhower even though I'd much rather marry you."

"Don't say such things. You're not in your right mind."

Kirkendale rose. Two steps later he'd closed the distance between them and captured her in his arms. "I know how I feel, Jessamine."

He kissed her in a gentle, teasing fashion, exploring her lips with his. Although Jessamine knew it was the drink which motivated Lord Kirkendale's desire, she made no attempt to pull away. Instead she pressed herself closer, deepening the kiss and losing herself in his embrace. *These few moments are all*

I will ever have of him. Please let it last a little longer! With clumsy desperation, Kirkendale pulled the pins from her hair. As it fell around her shoulders, he buried his face in the silky strands. "My beautiful Jessamine. Even your name is like poetry."

Abruptly, he released her and stepped back. He swayed toward her once more, his gaze resting on her lips. "Please tell me to leave before I do something you'll regret."

"You really should," she murmured. *Even though I'm not sure I would regret anything.*

"Just once before I go, say my name."

She reached up to stroke the angular curve of his cheekbone. "It's late, Dallas, and you need sleep."

He nodded, caught her hand, and kissed her palm. A mischievous smile curved his lips at the corners. "Ssh. This'll be our secret."

"I won't tell a soul."

After Kirkendale stumbled from the library, Jessamine was so stunned by what had occurred that she was rooted to the spot. If not for the fact he'd left his hat behind, she would have thought their interlude was a strange dream. Kirkendale had kissed her and called her beautiful, but under the circumstances only a naïf would believe he meant it. *What on Earth had driven the man to drink?*

Hairpins were scattered on the carpet at her feet. In a daze, she knelt to pick them up, but couldn't be sure if she'd found them all. *I'll check again tomorrow, in the daylight.* She carried Kirkendale's hat out of the library, left it on the entranceway table, and mounted the stairs to the third floor. *His Lordship will certainly not remember what transpired just now, but I'll never forget it.*

CHAPTER 9

DILEMMA

Daylight pressed in on Dallas's eyelids, making him nauseous. He heard Baum enter his room, humming under his breath, and the sound roiled his stomach further. Dallas tried to pull a pillow over his head to muffle the light and noise, but then he realized he'd fallen onto his bed sideways, fully clothed, with his pillow out of reach. *At least I remembered to remove my shoes.* He opened his eyes to discover his valet peering at him.

"First I'll draw you a bath. Then, I'll have Mrs. Crandall send up a pot of tea and some toast." Baum disappeared into the bathroom.

"Thank you." His voice sounded like a croak.

When he sat up, the room spun sideways. Parts of last night were a blank. After leaving the attorney's office, he had walked to his club and began to drink. Stansbury had joined him for part of the evening, that much he knew. What the attorney had told Dallas suddenly floated into his conscious-ness and hit him like a sledgehammer. *My sister was born in France, the illegitimate offspring of my father and some courtesan.*

My mother feigned pregnancy and pretended Amelie was hers. And if I don't keep Sir Bart happy he'll reveal what he knows and ruin Amelie's life. The secret was so awful, he couldn't tell anyone, ever. Did Olivia Hightower know, or Sir Bart's wife, Maud? Dallas had hoped to shake off the coil binding him to the Hightowers, but instead felt it tightening around his neck like a noose.

The sound of running water roused him from his reverie. Baum returned and helped him off with his clothes. "Why didn't you ring for me last night, sir? I would have been happy to get you ready for bed."

"I came in late and didn't want to disturb you." *I think.*

A few moments later he was soaking in a tub of hot water. *I'll never drink again to drown my sorrows.* Marriage to Olivia Hightower wouldn't be the end of the world, he reasoned. She could live here in London while he lived at Arbor Manor. Or perhaps if she preferred to be near her parents, it would be the other way around. Plenty of married couples almost never saw one another, and it worked out well. When it came time to sire an heir, he'd just have to do his duty. With a shudder, he ducked underneath the surface of the water until he was forced to come up for air. *Bloody Hell.*

Six months ago, he'd been fine with the state of things. Olivia wasn't unattractive. It wasn't like he didn't get along with her. Then Jessamine—Miss Foster—had come into his life. A wisp of a memory flashed into his throbbing brain...the sensation of her soft lips against his...and then the recollection slipped away. *I shouldn't drive myself crazy chasing the memory of something that never happened.*

When he emerged from the bathroom, wrapped in a robe, Baum had laid out a fresh change of clothes for the day. In addition, a tray with his tea and toast had been brought to his room. While his valet tidied up the bathroom, Dallas poured a cup of tea and waited for it to cool. His bloodshot eyes fell on a silver catch bowl filled with items emptied from his pockets. An unusual object drew his attention. *Why was a hairpin in my pocket?* He gasped as the memory of last night returned. *Oh, no! What have I done?*

Lord Kirkendale was absent when Jessamine and Amelie entered the dining room for breakfast. Jessamine drew a deep breath of relief as she was seated. Her plan was to behave as if nothing untoward had happened between her and her employer, but she was not ready to test her acting ability yet.

"I suppose Dallas drank too much and spent the night at his club," Amelie said.

"Perhaps. Is he in the habit of drinking a great deal?"

"I've never seen him drunk before, but there's always a first time."

Jessamine's hand shook as she sipped her tea, and a crease appeared between Amelie's eyebrows. "You seem quite unnerved this morning. Are you having trouble sleeping?"

"Oh…it's just that we have so much to do today," Jessamine replied. "Can we leave directly after breakfast? I'd like to visit the milliners before the morning crush."

"Certainly."

"Perhaps you'd like to lunch at the Savoy today?"

"That would be marvelous! I'll let Mrs. Crandall know."

After she finished her breakfast, Amelie went upstairs to get her hat, gloves, and reticule. Jessamine crept up the servants' staircase to the third floor to do the same. Then she waited in the foyer, where Lord Kirkendale's hat was still resting on the table. Amelie noticed the hat as she descended the stairs.

"So Dallas slept here after all," she said.

The butler appeared. "Your carriage is ready, milady."

"Thank you, Mr. DeVane. Will you inform Lord Kirkendale and Mrs. Crandall we'll be out for lunch?"

"Very good, milady."

Jessamine whisked Amelie out the door and managed to keep her away from the house most of the day. On the drive back to Eaton Square, she noticed footmen from Arbor Manor outside the Fosters' townhouse, carrying a trunk inside from a mountain of baggage on the sidewalk.

"It seems my relatives have come to town," Jessamine murmured.

Amelie leaned toward the window and stuck out her tongue. "Go home!"

"That's not the kind of behavior a properly brought up young lady ought be exhibiting!" Despite her words, Jessamine bit back a smile. Truth be told, she'd been tempted to stick her tongue out as well.

Mid-morning, Dallas and Stansbury met for a ride on Rotten Row. Stansbury smirked at his appearance. "You look a bit worse for wear."

"Thanks."

"I've rarely seen you drink like you did last night," Stansbury said. "I'm surprised you feel up to riding."

"I don't much feel like it, but I need the exercise," Dallas replied. "And the drinking was because I came to a decision yesterday."

"A decision as to what, exactly?"

"I'm going to marry Olivia Hightower."

"I assume you discovered there was no way around it?"

"No, and I would ask you not to press me on the matter."

A crowd of people had formed up ahead, craning their necks toward the riding track. A handsome well-dressed woman appeared, driving a smart cabriolet. The onlookers smiled and waved as she approached, perhaps hoping to attract a smile from the woman's full lips. To Stansbury's obvious amusement, Dallas stared along with everyone else. After she passed, the crowd began to disperse.

"Who was that woman?"

"The Paris Lilly," Stansbury replied. "She's been mistress to the most powerful men in Europe, or so they say. You wouldn't be the first to fancy her."

"I don't fancy her. I just felt as if I'd seen her somewhere before."

Dallas urged his mount forward. He and Stansbury trotted along for a while until they were obliged to slow for a knot of other riders.

"Perhaps I can coax you, Miss Foster, and Amelie to the theater tonight," Stansbury said. "I've come into four tickets to a musical review." He paused. "Oh, no."

"What's the matter?"

"I see Miss Hightower up ahead. That's bad luck."

Dallas raised his hand to wave, and Olivia gave him a beaming smile. His heart heavy, he brought his horse to a halt alongside her and lifted his hat. "Good morning, Miss Hightower. You remember my friend Lord Stansbury?"

"Of course," Olivia said. "Good morning, gentlemen."

Dallas cleared his throat. "If you're free this evening, would you care to accompany my sister, Stansbury, and me to the theater?"

Out of the corner of his eye, Dallas noticed Stansbury blanch.

"Why, I would be delighted," Olivia replied. "I always adore spending time with your sister."

"Let's dine out beforehand," Dallas said. "We'll swing by in the carriage to pick you up at six o'clock. Would that suit you?"

"I'd like nothing better."

WHEN JESSAMINE and Amelie arrived at the townhouse, Amelie summoned footmen to carry the packages still in the carriage. Kirkendale appeared in the doorway of the drawing room.

"Oh hello, Dallas," Amelie said. "I feel like I haven't seen you for ages."

"You're just in time for tea. Please join me."

"Excuse me, Your Lordship, but I'm a little tired. I think I'll lie down before dinner," Jessamine said.

His gaze was unflinching, but his voice was kind. "If you wish, but Lady Amelie and I are going out for dinner tonight. I must speak with you before then."

A heated flush spread across Jessamine's face. *Does he remember?*

"Thank you, sir. I'll be right down," she managed.

Jessamine mounted the stairs and returned to her room. As she tidied her appearance, her heart was racing and her palms became moist. *If Lord Kirkendale remembers what happened between us, how am I to behave?*

ALTHOUGH HE PRETENDED to listen to Amelie talk about the day's activities, Dallas had been unsettled by the sight of Miss Foster. Although his recollection was fuzzy, he remembered the taste of her kiss and the intoxicating fragrance of her hair.

"You're not listening to me at all," Amelie said finally.

"Oh yes, I am. I heard every word."

"I just told you I bought a giraffe for the garden and you didn't say anything."

"I, uh, assumed you were joking."

"So why are we going out for dinner tonight?"

"Stansbury and Olivia are dining with us, and afterward the four of us will attend a musical review."

His sister slumped back onto the sofa. "Oh."

"I thought you'd be delighted."

"I'd be more delighted if we were going with Jessamine."

"It's time you get to know Miss Hightower better. She and I will be announcing our engagement soon."

Pink spots appeared on Amelie's cheeks, and she set her teacup down with a crash.

"I don't want you to marry that cow! I want you to marry Jessamine!"

The breath nearly left his body. *If only Amelie realized how badly I want to do exactly that.* "I'm afraid marriage to Miss Foster isn't in the cards."

Amelie stood. "I'll be in my room until it's time to leave."

Jessamine lingered upstairs as long as she dared, then descended the stairs to the drawing room. She anticipated hearing Amelie's happy conversation flowing through the open door, but silence greeted her instead. *Perhaps they gave me up as a lost cause and are in their rooms dressing for dinner?* A tentative peek inside the drawing room, however, revealed Lord Kirkendale standing next to the fireplace.

"Milord, you wished to speak with me?"

His lost and vulnerable expression made Jessamine's heart melt. *What could be troubling him so?*

"Please come in and shut the door."

Mystified, she did as he asked. Lord Kirkendale remained standing as she approached, his face becoming increasingly cloudy. He crossed over to meet her and held something out for her to take. "I found this in my pocket this morning."

A hairpin. A sense of relief loosened the muscles in her shoulders as she took the pin from him. "Thank you very much, milord. I must have dropped it somewhere, but I can't imagine how it ended up in your pocket!"

"You don't have to pretend."

Her smile faded. "I'm sorry, but I don't understand."

"I owe you an apology for my boorish behavior, Miss Foster. I admit I was completely in the wrong. Some bad news yesterday drove me over the edge, and I showed you a side of me I would rather stay hidden."

He regrets kissing me and the things he said. "You needn't speak of it again. It will be forgotten in due course." To her horror, her throat began to close up and her eyelids began to sting with emotion.

"I-I can't employ you any longer. You can comprehend the dilemma, I hope? It wouldn't be fair to you with the both of us living under the same roof."

She cursed the tear that dribbled down the side of her face, turning away so he couldn't notice.

"I'll provide you with a glowing reference, of course, and furnish you with six months' wages to compensate you for the inconvenience of having to look for another position," he continued. "And you needn't resort to replying to advertisements. I'll contact a reputable employment agency on your behalf."

The hairpin in Jessamine's hand dug into her palm as she

edged backward toward the door. "Thank you, sir. You've been very kind." Her voice quavered, and she bit the inside of her cheek to maintain her composure.

"Damn it, Jessamine, it can't be helped!"

Kirkendale's voice had a quaver in it too, but she would not look at him. She fled the drawing room without a backward glance.

Enveloped in a maelstrom of emotions, Jessamine shut herself up in her room and sobbed. Mixed in with the grief and regret was also a renewed and exquisitely painful sensation of abandonment. *My parents left me all alone. The Fosters didn't want me around. I'm unwelcome in Lord Kirkendale's life. There's something horribly wrong with me.*

When she did not appear downstairs for dinner, one of the maids tapped on her door.

"I'm unwell," Jessamine called out. "I don't want anything to eat." Her throat was so raw from crying, she did sound ill. The maid went away, and Jessamine collapsed on the floor in a heap. She tried to tell herself that self-pity wasn't helping the situation, but she felt like she was fifteen years old again, newly orphaned and scared out of her wits.

Fear eventually gave way to anger. *Lord Kirkendale took advantage of my weakness. Obviously I'm one in a long string of girls to suffer the same fate. He drew me in, made me care, and has now discarded me. Will he hire another companion for his sister now?* A fresh round of tears fell as grief supplanted the anger. Amelie possessed such a free spirit, Jessamine could hardly bear to be parted from her. How was she to say good-bye, and what reason would she give for her departure?

It was after two in the morning when Jessamine dragged

herself off the floor and washed her face in the basin. She lay down on her bed but could only doze for a few minutes at a time. Finally she gave up and just stared at the canopy overhead. The thought of returning to the Fosters until she secured another position was insupportable. No matter what reference Lord Kirkendale gave her, they would assume she'd been sacked. *Charlotte and Aunt Rachel will mock me openly. It was folly to have taken this position, but in my arrogance I thought I could succeed where others had failed. What a fool I am to have given my heart away so easily.*

CHAPTER 10
TREACHERY

As Dallas and Amelie sat down to breakfast, one of the maids brought word that Miss Foster was unwell and would not be coming down. A fresh wave of regret swept over Dallas.

"See that a tray is brought to her room," he said.

The maid curtsied. "Yes, sir."

"Poor Jessamine," Amelie said after the maid left. "I'll go check on her after breakfast. Yesterday she seemed perfectly well."

Since all the servants were out of the room, Dallas decided to broach the subject of Miss Foster's termination. "Her absence probably has nothing to do with illness. Yesterday afternoon I told her she must seek other employment."

"What?" Amelie's body grew rigid. "Is this Olivia's doing?"

"No. I decided Miss Foster's presence in this house was unwise."

"Because you're in love with her?"

Dallas stared at his sister, startled. "Where did you get that idea?"

"You have a puppy dog expression every time you look at her."

"In point of fact, I have feelings that aren't appropriate considering her status in this household," he admitted. "She's blameless, of course. I'm giving her a generous severance and a letter of reference."

"How *could* you? Send for Jessamine right now and tell her you've changed your mind."

"I can't do that. Some things just aren't meant to be."

"Why not? What is so important about Olivia that you have to marry her?"

"Papa arranged it."

"To hell with Papa and to hell with you."

Amelie stormed out. Although he knew he ought to correct her for her language, he merely dropped his head in his hands. *I agree with her. To hell with Papa and me both.*

Jessamine sat at her dressing table, forlorn, while Amelie used a hairbrush to work out the tangles in her hair. An untouched breakfast tray rested on a table nearby.

"There must be some way around this," Amelie said.

"I think not," Jessamine said. "Your brother will contact an employment agency on my behalf later today and I'll likely take the first position offered."

"Make sure it's in London. That way we can at least see each other."

"I daresay it will be abroad, if the advertisements I saw last time are any indication. And perhaps that's for the best. I'm not sure if I can bear to see Lord Kirkendale again."

"Do you hate him now?"

Jessamine's eyes filled with tears, but she shook her head.

"I'm angry with him, Amelie, but I can't hate him. I'm probably angrier at myself for not marshaling my feelings more stridently."

"So you *do* have feelings for him?"

"He's intelligent, kind, handsome, charming, and possesses something in his manner that women find irresistible. I'm no exception."

Amelie reached for a poppy-seed muffin. "There must be a way to get you two together," she exclaimed through a mouthful of pastry. "Dallas cares for you as well."

The memory of his kisses made Jessamine tear up again. "If he has made promises to Miss Hightower, as a gentleman he must keep them." She pulled her hair forward and began to twist it into a braid.

"He hasn't promised Olivia anything. Our father arranged it before he died, or so Dallas tells me. I can't fathom why. This is the twentieth century! Nobody enters into arranged marriages anymore. Oh, he makes me so angry!"

Despite her own misery, Jessamine didn't want to cause a rift between Amelie and Lord Kirkendale. "Your brother's focus on your welfare does him credit. I've no money and no connections. He understands full well if he made an alliance with me it would be detrimental to your chance to make a good match."

"My parents made a good match and they couldn't abide one another! I want love and romance."

"Should you make a misstep in Society, the man you fall in love with may be prevented from returning your feelings. You don't want to find yourself in the same cruel situation as I do."

"Any man who would not want you for a sister-in-law is not the sort of man I would marry."

"You are the sweetest girl, Amelie. Take heart; Miss Hightower may grow on you in due course. Don't let your regard for me poison your opinion of her."

"The poison is all Olivia's, I assure you. There's something sly about her, and I have reason to believe she caused all my governesses to leave."

"That's a very strong accusation, Amelie. Why would you say such a thing?"

"Before my last governess left, I happened to see Olivia Hightower walking with her. That happened twice before, and both governesses left their positions shortly thereafter without notice."

"Perhaps Miss Hightower merely enjoyed their company?"

"You don't know Olivia as well as I do. She would never willingly socialize with anyone not on her level."

"Did you say anything to Lord Kirkendale about this?"

"Since I was delighted at their departure, no. Perhaps—"

A tap on the door interrupted Amelie's reply. Maureen was in the hallway, wearing her usual sullen expression. "You've a caller in the drawing room, Miss Foster."

Bewildered, Jessamine peered at her. "Who could be calling for me?"

"Your uncle, Mr. Thackery Foster."

Jessamine's heart sank. "I'll be right down." *Lord Kirkendale must have sent for him. He cannot be rid of me fast enough.*

DALLAS REALIZED he was scowling at Mr. Foster, but he had no reason to do otherwise. *The nerve of the man, showing his face here!*

"Miss Foster is a lovely lady, sir, and my sister and I count ourselves quite fortunate to have her in our employ. I cannot fathom, however, why she's not preparing for her Season along with your own daughter."

A florid stain crept across Mr. Foster's cheekbones. "It's all been a dreadful misunderstanding, Lord Kirkendale, and one that I mean to remedy forthwith."

"A misunderstanding? In what way?"

"There was some, er, friction in my household of which I was unaware. You know how ladies can be."

"You admit you don't know what transpires under your own roof?"

"Yes, well, business in London called me away frequently. Too frequently, as it turned out."

"And yet you've had no contact with Miss Foster since she's been working for me."

"Inexcusable, I admit, but things are in hand now. I hope Jessamine will forgive me and return home. Perhaps some encouragement from you in that regard would be helpful."

"I've no reason to assist you, sir. I only want what's best for Miss Foster."

Amelie entered the drawing room, followed shortly thereafter by a wan Miss Foster. Dallas knew he was the cause of the deep shadows underneath Miss Foster's beautiful eyes, and he longed to comfort her somehow. *There's nothing I wouldn't do to make her happy again.* "Hello, Uncle Thackery," she said.

"Jessamine, it's good to see you."

"Amelie, allow me to introduce my uncle, Mr. Foster. Uncle Thackery, this is Lady Amelie Marsden." Miss Foster's tone was restrained. "I see you've already met Lord Kirkendale."

"Yes, he's been most gracious. Good morning, Lady Amelie," Mr. Foster said.

The man took a half-step toward his niece as if to embrace her, but Miss Foster immediately sat on the sofa alongside Amelie. His sister's jaw was set in a stubborn line Dallas knew all too well. *I pity Mr. Foster, should he say one wrong word.*

"Er, I've come to escort you home, Jessamine. I made a dreadful mistake by allowing your aunt too free a hand in your management. I'm prepared to give you a generous allowance to prepare for the Season ahead."

Miss Foster peered at her uncle. "How did you know where to find me?"

He turned pale, and his eyes darted toward Dallas and Amelie. *The man is hiding something.*

"That's not important right now," Mr. Foster said. "What's important is that your aunt, cousin, and I are prepared to make amends. You shall have the Season your parents intended."

A tear glistened on Miss Foster's cheek. "And what if I don't want to?"

Something like panic flickered across Mr. Foster's face. "I, er, would implore you to think about your future, Jessamine."

"I think you should consider it, Miss Foster," Dallas said. "In fact, I insist."

"Dallas!" Amelie exclaimed.

Jessamine fixed him with a wounded gaze. "Of course. Forgive me, sir. I'd forgotten your wish that I should depart this house as soon as possible."

"Miss Foster, you misunderstand. If you don't leave here, I won't have the opportunity to court you properly."

A stunned silence ensued, followed by Amelie's delighted gasp. Dallas was no less taken aback by his sudden declaration, but he had no wish to retract it. *I want to marry Jessamine, whatever the cost. May God help Sir Bart if he chooses to besmirch my family name. I'll deny his assertions, and nobody can prove otherwise. He will look like a lying fool.*

At first Jessamine thought she hadn't heard Lord Kirkendale correctly. *He wants to court me?* She searched his face for confirmation, and the gentle smile on his lips warmed her from the inside out. "I thought your intentions lay in another direction," she said.

"My interest has been unwavering, I can assure you, but not toward Miss Hightower. I've decided I can no longer allow my father to control my life from the grave."

"Bravo!" Amelie exclaimed.

"In that case, Uncle Thackery, I will accompany you willingly." Miss Foster rose from the sofa. "I'll pack a few things and return directly. Perhaps we can send the footmen to retrieve the rest."

As Jessamine left the drawing room, Amelie danced alongside her. "I knew it would work out!" she whispered as they climbed the stairs. "Dallas has come to his senses at last. You and I will become sisters."

Although it was nearly impossible, Jessamine held in her emotions until she reached her room. Then she gave her friend a big hug. "Oh, Amelie, my heart is overflowing with happiness! I've had no hope for so long...and now this!"

"As soon as you're settled, we'll resume our shopping," Amelie said. "It will be your turn to shop for fetching garments to quicken Dallas's blood."

"Amelie!"

They burst out laughing. This time, the moisture in Jessamine's eyes were tears of joy. Finally, she retrieved a tapestry bag from the wardrobe and began to collect her toiletries and personal belongings.

"I'm only sorry you'll be living with the Fosters from now on," Amelie said as Jessamine packed. "Your uncle seems all right, I suppose."

"I'll spend every moment possible out of their house. When the Season starts in earnest, I daresay Aunt Rachel and cousin Charlotte will be otherwise occupied. I'm certain I can bear up under the deprivation."

Her activity was interrupted by a soft tapping at the door. Amelie opened it. "What are you doing here, Dallas?"

"I want to have a word with Miss Foster," Kirkendale said.

"Not in her bedroom you won't," Amelie said. "It isn't proper."

Kirkendale made a sound of exasperation and jerked his head toward the hall. "Scat. Five minutes alone won't cause tongues to wag, especially if nobody knows."

With a giggle and a wink at Jessamine, Amelie left. In Kirkendale's presence, Jessamine suddenly became tongue-tied. He rested his hands on her shoulders.

"I hope I haven't been presumptuous," he said. "If so, tell me now."

"You have not, Your Lordship."

He pulled her into an embrace. "Call me Dallas."

She tilted her head back to receive his kiss, and reveled in the heat his lips aroused. This time he tasted of strawberries and passion, and she didn't want him to stop. She cared for him, deeply, and now that she knew he returned her affection, she wasn't afraid to show it. She answered his passion with her own, and only a subtle cough at the door made her come to her senses.

"It's been six minutes," Amelie said. "The flies on the wall are beginning to talk."

Dallas deposited one final kiss on Jessamine's forehead and stepped away. He shot his sister a level look. "I had no idea you were to be such an overbearing chaperone, Amelie."

She tossed her head. "And I had no idea of you ever needing one. It seems we must both adjust."

〜

UNLIKE ARBOR MANOR, the Foster's London townhouse had not been redecorated. As Jessamine stepped through the door, it was almost like stepping back in time. In addition, beloved servants rushed to greet her, including Hannah. Jessamine returned their greetings warmly and gave Hannah a hug.

"I never gave up hope, Miss Jessamine," the maid murmured.

Mrs. Foster and Charlotte appeared in the doorway of the drawing room.

"How lovely to have you back, dear." Mrs. Foster's smile was as brittle as ice.

"It's good of you to have me." Jessamine's sentiment was politeness only. *Undoubtedly Aunt Rachel's objections to my return were overridden.*

"Hello, Jessamine," Charlotte cooed.

Charlotte's syrupy sweet tone nearly made Jessamine gag. In addition, she was startled by the maliciousness radiating from her cousin's eyes. *I knew she and Aunt Rachel disliked me, but I hadn't thought it had turned to hatred. Something odd has happened since I saw them last.*

"Well, well, this is a touching reunion," Mr. Foster said. "Hannah, will you show Jessamine upstairs?"

"Yes, sir."

Hannah led her to one of the spare rooms and closed the door. "I probably ought to keep this to myself, but I think you have the right to know. Your Aunt Lillian arranged your return to the Fosters."

"What?"

Hannah quickly filled Jessamine in on Aunt Lillian's visit to Arbor Manor and what she'd said. "The servants talked amongst ourselves afterward, and we learned Eugene had been nicking Miss Perrisham's letters at Mrs. Foster's request.

Although Eugene couldn't be completely sure, he believed the letters contained money."

Jessamine gasped. "I had not thought my aunt as bad as that!"

"In the beginning, Mrs. Foster told him the correspondence was from an unwelcome admirer. She's been paying him the last three years to nick the letters."

"No!"

"After Mr. Foster found out what had been happening under his own nose, he got his dander up. I'd say he put the fear of God into Mrs. Foster."

"Now I understand why Aunt Rachel glared at me the way she did." Jessamine paused. "Will she give me my letters now?"

"I overheard her tell Mr. Foster she'd burned every one of them."

Pain stabbed at Jessamine's temples as she'd realized the extent of Aunt Rachel's treachery.

"I'm grateful Aunt Lillian played the part of the avenging angel on my behalf. I must thank her in person."

"Oh, no! Miss Perrisham insisted you keep your distance. Although she looks and behaves like a perfect lady, she's demi-monde." Hannah whispered the last word as if it pained her to say it. "I hope I haven't shocked you."

"Actually, I'm not surprised by the revelation. Mr. Oakley mentioned something about it before. One thing confuses me, though. How did Aunt Lillian learn I was working for Lord Kirkendale in the first place?"

CHAPTER II
LA MAD MODISTE

Laden with packages, Olivia and her mother entered their Pimlico townhouse. Sir Bart emerged from the drawing room with a glass of spirits in one hand and a letter in the other. His color was high and his gait unsteady.

"Been spending more of my money, I see."

"Oh, hello, Papa," Olivia said.

"Good morning, dear." Lady Hightower gave her husband a peck on the cheek. "When did you arrive?"

"An hour ago."

"If I'd known you were coming, I would have sent the carriage to the station for you."

"Thanks to your daughter, we may not be able to keep a carriage much longer!"

Sir Bart turned on his heel and retreated into the drawing room. Olivia exchanged a bewildered glance with Lady Hightower before they followed.

"What are you speaking of, Papa?" Olivia asked.

"I've heard from Lord Kirkendale." He waved the letter in the air. "Not only is he repudiating any notion of marriage to you, but he has severed our business relationship as well! Without his horses to trade, we are ruined."

Lady Hightower gasped and fixed her stunned daughter with an accusing glare. "Why didn't you tell me you'd given offense?"

"I haven't! When Dallas escorted me to dinner and the theater with Amelie and Stansbury, our conversation was congenial!" Olivia frowned. "This must have something to do with that scheming companion, Miss Foster."

"What the devil does she have to do with it?" Sir Bart asked.

"She has designs on Dallas, of course." Olivia raised an eyebrow. "Are you going to retaliate?"

"Retaliate?" Lady Hightower glanced from Olivia to Sir Bart, confused. "Whatever does she mean?"

"Only that Papa has been blackmailing the Marsden family for years, going back to the Sixth Earl of Kirkendale," Olivia snapped.

Lady Hightower's eyes rolled upward, and she swayed on her feet. "I may faint."

Sir Bart helped his wife over to a sofa where she promptly swooned. Olivia made a sound of disgust at her mother's weakness.

"What are you prepared to do?" she demanded as her father rang for a servant.

"Truth be told, there's not much I can do. With Phillip Marsden dead, I've no real proof anymore what transpired eighteen years ago. His son has called my bluff and we shall very shortly be obliged to sell our assets."

"What secret were you holding over Lord Kirkendale's head?"

"Never mind that now. You'd best marry the richest man you can find, Olivia, and quickly. Otherwise, you'll end up working as a servant like Miss Foster."

Sir Bart sank down onto the sofa next to Lady Hightower and rested his face in his hands. Olivia was glad he couldn't see the scorn in her heart. *My father may have given up, but revenge is mine. If Dallas has thrown me over for Jessamine Foster, I'll strike him where it hurts most.*

Mrs. Foster and Charlotte radiated hostility toward Jessamine over dinner and froze her out of the conversation as much as possible. The atmosphere was so unpleasant and unwelcoming, Jessamine found it difficult to choke down her food. As her cousin and aunt prattled on about Charlotte's debutante reception scheduled in May, Jessamine kept her gaze focused on her roast chicken.

"Excuse me, Mrs. Foster, but Jessamine is to share the spotlight at the reception," Mr. Foster said finally. "Have you included her in your plans?"

Sharklike, Mrs. Foster's teeth gleamed in the light from the chandelier overhead.

"Perhaps Jessamine has made some acquaintances during her employment she would like to invite?"

The edge of sarcasm in her tone was obvious, and Charlotte didn't bother to hide her snicker. Although Jessamine sighed inwardly, she was unfazed. "Actually, I would like to extend an invitation to Lord Kirkendale and his sister, Lady Amelie Marsden."

"An earl and his family? Do you really believe they would attend?" Mrs. Foster scoffed.

"Lord Kirkendale has already declared his interest in courting our Jessamine," Mr. Foster said.

Charlotte knocked over her glass of water, and servants

rushed to mop up the spill. Her cool gaze settled on Jessamine. "Fast work, cousin. I suppose it's in your blood."

My blood? "What does that mean?"

"Nothing at all." She shrugged. "It's just that some girls draw men in with easy virtue. Whether they can lead them to the altar thereafter is another matter."

Ordinarily inured to Charlotte's digs, Jessamine was caught off guard by her cousin's shocking lack of manners. "I'm offended at your implication."

"You spent weeks under the earl's roof, and I've heard he's a very handsome man. I'm not the only one who will assume an illicit liaison occurred."

"Charlotte, if you can't keep a civil tongue you may be excused," Mr. Foster said.

Instead of being brought up short by her father's reprimand, Charlotte merely folded her napkin and gave Jessamine a secretive smile. As Charlotte left the dining room, Mrs. Foster pouted.

"I wish you hadn't sent her away, Mr. Foster," Mrs. Foster said. "Charlotte and I had much to discuss."

"Now that the Season is upon us, you have just as much to discuss with Jessamine," he said. "Now is your opportunity."

An ugly expression distorted Mrs. Foster's features. "I believe I've developed a sudden headache." She rose and sailed from the room.

Mr. Foster rubbed his eyes with his thumb and forefinger, giving Jessamine an apologetic smile afterward. "I'll see that the invitation is sent to your friends, even if I have to deliver it personally."

"Thank you." She paused. "Uncle, please let's not pretend this situation is a happy one for any of us. I understand my Great-Aunt Lillian is responsible for my return."

"Who told you? If it was Charlotte, I'll—"

"No, it was Hannah. Please don't blame her. I couldn't imagine it being Aunt Rachel's idea."

"Nor mine, I'm ashamed to say. Jessamine, I deserve your rebuke. I should have taken better care of you, but I allowed my attention to be drawn elsewhere. I cannot forgive myself."

"Don't blame yourself, Uncle. If I hadn't left Arbor Manor, I wouldn't have met Lord Kirkendale or Lady Amelie. Knowing them has enriched my life more than I would have thought possible."

When Mr. Foster smiled, the crinkles around the corner of his eyes reminded Jessamine of her father. He even reached across the table and patted her hand as her father would have done. "I wish you every happiness, my dear."

"Do you have Aunt Lillian's address so I may send her a letter? I don't want her to think I'm not grateful for her assistance."

"It's in my study. I almost forgot, Miss Perrisham made an appointment for you with her own modiste tomorrow morning." Mr. Foster reached for his glass of wine. "She's a formidable woman, your aunt."

MADEMOISELLE MADELEINE LEGRANGE was a modiste so exclusive that only an understated metal plaque with *La Mad Modiste* appeared on the side of the building. The entrance was located down a private alley, away from prying eyes. Although Jessamine had heard of Mademoiselle LeGrange, she never expected to become one of her clientele. None but the highest echelon of Society could hope to book an appointment at her establishment, and those slots were given months in advance.

A fashionably-dressed assistant named Veronique welcomed Jessamine into the shop and greeted her by name.

After pressing a flute of champagne into Jessamine's hand, she whisked her down a long hallway to a large private sitting room. A rack of garments fashioned from all manner of delectable fabrics was positioned next to a mirrored alcove and a dressing screen. Jessamine abandoned her champagne on a table and crossed over to admire the dresses.

"*Magnifique, non?*" Veronique asked.

"*Oui,*" Jessamine replied. "*Absolument.*"

Just as she reached out to touch a gown decorated with an overlay of gold netting, a petite older woman strode into the room, radiating the energy of a small tornado. She circled Jessamine once, examining her from head to toe, and then reeled off instructions to her assistant in French. Veronique lifted a white debutante gown from the rack and held it up. "Mademoiselle LeGrange wishes to begin your fitting with this one."

Jessamine gaped in amazement. Except for a difference in the neckline, the pleating, and the placement of the beads, the gown was almost an exact copy of her mother's debutante gown.

"How—"

"That was *my* debutante gown," a woman's voice said. "I thought perhaps you might like to have it."

A striking woman with dark hair and blue eyes had entered the room and came around to face Jessamine. "Minerva and I wanted to wear the exact same dress, but our mothers insisted on a few differences."

"Aunt Lillian?" Finally face to face with her great-aunt, Jessamine wasn't certain how to behave. It was very difficult to ignore the fact that the woman was demimonde...and yet she'd been very kind and generous. *I must try not to judge.*

"Call me Lilly, please."

When Jessamine gave Lilly an impulsive kiss on the

cheek, tears pooled in the woman's eyes. As she stared, Jessamine flashed back to her parent's funeral. "You were at the church service for my parents...sitting by yourself in the back."

Lilly seemed startled. "I can't believe you remember that."

"I didn't until just now."

"I wanted to speak with you then, but I didn't dare." Lilly's gaze slid to Veronique and Mademoiselle LeGrange. "We'll talk later. Right now it's time to turn you into a trendsetter."

OUT OF SORTS and anxious about her future, Olivia rose early to dress for a ladies' breakfast. She'd recently told several friends about her pending engagement to Dallas, and would now have to gracefully retract it. Although she intended to spin the details to her advantage, she hated losing the admiration and expressions of envy she'd enjoyed as Lord Kirkendale's future fiancée. The best she could hope for would be to distract her friends from their pity by setting her sights on another eligible target as quickly as possible.

Several young debutantes were among the party guests. Olivia gritted her teeth as she was introduced to the fresh-faced girls who were to vie with each other—and her—for available husbands that Season. *I will have to lower the necklines of my ball gowns.* When she was introduced to Miss Charlotte Foster, she had to marshal her countenance. *She's not nearly as handsome as her cousin!* Fortunately, Miss Foster and Olivia weren't seated at the same table. *If I have to make conversation with her, I'll be sick.*

As gossip ebbed and flowed, Olivia finally received the pointed question she'd been dreading.

"I understand you may soon be announcing your engage

ment to an earl, Miss Hightower? Please don't keep us in suspense."

Although she'd planned a campaign to destroy Jessamine Foster's reputation, Olivia could scarcely do so with the woman's cousin in the room. So she settled for a coy smile and a deflection. *I can always fill in the details later, in private...that Lord Kirkendale is consorting with the niece of a known prostitute.* "While it's true the gentleman has been pressing me to make the announcement, I'm afraid my affections have cooled somewhat."

"No!"

"Don't be silly! Let your affections cool after you are married."

A forced laugh was Olivia's response. "Marriage is forever, as you know, so I'm in no rush. Truthfully, I've been yearning to travel. Perhaps I'll set sail for America and marry a rich industrialist."

"But Americans are so vulgar, my dear. If you're determined to marry a foreigner, let it be a Canadian. Or find yourself a German with a title. German royalty, at least, have a certain cachet."

As the conversation turned to which foreign accent was the most grating, Olivia was relieved to be out of the spotlight for the moment. She was under no illusion, however, that her aborted engagement wouldn't be a hot topic behind her back.

To Olivia's displeasure, Miss Charlotte Foster was waiting to speak with her after the party was over. "Forgive my impertinence, Miss Hightower, but I heard your plans to marry Lord Kirkendale have come to naught?"

Olivia did her best to freeze the chit with a glance. "I cannot believe you would listen to idle gossip, Miss Foster. Good day to you."

The girl caught Olivia's arm as she brushed past. "Should

you ever seek revenge, I can help. In fact, perhaps we can help each other."

Instantly suspicious, Olivia narrowed her eyes. "In what way?"

"I've come into possession of some old letters. If their contents were known, it would ruin my cousin Jessamine completely."

"Why would you want to do that?"

"Because she's not my cousin at all."

CHAPTER 12
RUDE AWAKENINGS

Lilly gave Jessamine a ride back to Eaton Square in her own carriage. Jessamine was in a delirious haze of contentment. Although most of her wardrobe would not be ready for days, the seamstresses had managed to finish a few garments while she and her aunt shopped. She'd donned one of the exquisite tea gowns for the ride home, and reveled in her newfound confidence.

"My lady's maid performed miracles for me with Mama's old gowns, but having something of my own is absolutely wonderful." Jessamine's fingers slid over the sumptuous fabric of the skirt. "I've never dreamt of wearing anything so incredible."

"Mademoiselle LeGrange is the best, to be sure, but a shopping trip to Paris would not go amiss," Lilly said. "The gossip value of a Worth original is worth its price in gold."

Jessamine giggled. "I'll happily leave the gossip to those ladies who enjoy it. As long as I have Lord Kirkendale, I am satisfied."

As the carriage approached the Foster's townhouse, Lilly

retrieved her calling card and slipped it into Jessamine's hand. "If you ever need me, I'll be there for you, but you must be very careful not to mention our relationship to anyone other than the Fosters. Your Christian attitude toward me is commendable, but it will be shared by few others. I don't want you tainted by association with a courtesan, especially on the eve of your first Season."

"So I'm to profit from your generosity, but not admit any family connection? That sounds ugly and self-centered."

"Nevertheless, you know I'm right. Let nothing jeopardize your courtship with Lord Kirkendale." Lilly patted her hand. "Don't worry. I'm used to functioning outside Society, and I do it quite well."

"Will I see you again soon?"

"Any contact between us must be carefully managed, I'm afraid."

The carriage came to a stop. After giving her aunt a quick embrace, Jessamine stepped to the sidewalk and went into the house. Mr. Hattley relieved her of her shopping bag.

"Lady Amelie Marsden and Lord Kirkendale are awaiting you in the drawing room, Miss Jessamine."

OLIVIA GLANCED up when she finished reading the yellowed letter Miss Charlotte Foster had thrust into her hands minutes before. "As pitiable as these events are for the author, what have they to do with Jessamine Foster?"

Charlotte unfolded a second letter and gave to her. "This one is dated a few months later. Read on."

Dubious, Olivia skimmed the missive. Her sudden gasp was followed by a chortle. "Oh, this is too delicious for words."

Her young visitor smirked. "I thought you might enjoy it."

She glanced at the large packet of letters on the sofa next to her. "The other letters make interesting reading as well."

"How did you come upon them?"

"They were in a box of mementos Jessamine left at Arbor Manor when she went to work for Lord Kirkendale."

"I am acquainted with a certain newspaper publisher who might be interested in publishing these letters. Do I have your permission to sell them?"

"I don't care what you do with the letters. Once they've been published, I'll blame her lady's maid for the theft."

"If I may ask, why do you hate your cousin so much?"

"I'm sick of being compared to someone who's not related to me at all. Everyone has always told me how pretty Jessamine is, but I've always known there was something unwholesome about her. Now everyone else will know too."

After Charlotte left, Lady Hightower tottered down the stairs. "Who was your little friend, Olivia? Why didn't she stay for tea?"

The woman hiccupped into her handkerchief. Olivia could smell the port on her mother's breath. *At this rate, Mama and Papa will deplete the wine cellar in days!*

"She was nobody important," Olivia replied, dismissively. "Why don't you go back to your room and I'll have a tea tray sent up?"

"Aren't you having any tea?"

"Yes, but I'd rather be alone." Her fingers tightened on the packet of letters in her hand. "I have some reading to do."

AMELIE SQUEALED at the sight of Jessamine clad in her new finery. "You look so beautiful I almost didn't recognize you. You could be mistaken for one of the royal family!"

Jessamine laughed. "I don't know about that, but thank you." Her eyes slid to Lord Kirkendale. The admiration in his eyes sent a wave of pleasure down her spine, and his splendid appearance made her breath catch in her throat.

"I agree with my sister," he said. "You look like a princess."

Mrs. Foster's nostril flared with distaste. "I'll have tea sent in."

"Are Charlotte and Uncle Thackery coming down?" Jessamine asked.

"Your uncle is at his club and your cousin is paying a call. Excuse me, but I have business with my housekeeper."

The atmosphere in the room lightened as the woman left. Amelie settled herself on a sofa, so Jessamine took the spot next to her.

"Why didn't you wait to go shopping with me?" Amelie exclaimed.

"An old friend of my mother's arranged an appointment with Mademoiselle LeGrange at the last moment," Jessamine replied. "I couldn't refuse."

Lord Kirkendale's brows rose. "La Mad Modiste? Your mother's friend must be exceedingly well-connected."

Jessamine felt a flush warm her cheeks. "I believe she is."

Amelie gesticulated to her brother. "Give her the invitation, Dallas!"

He withdrew a heavy cream-colored envelope from his breast pocket and set it on the table. "You're to be our special guest at Amelie's ball in a fortnight. Assuming you're available of course."

"I wouldn't miss it for anything," Jessamine said.

"Good. I can't wait to dance with you again." Kirkendale had a twinkle in his eyes.

"Dallas and I are going riding with Stansbury tomorrow morning before breakfast. Would you be game?" Amelie asked.

"I'd adore it."

One of the maids brought in the tea cart, and Jessamine sighed with happiness. *I'm so blessed.*

As Dallas drank a glass of Irish whiskey and soaked in the masculine atmosphere of Boodles, he felt his shoulders relax. "I'm so happy to finally get a little peace," Dallas said. "All Amelie has talked about for the past two weeks is her debutante ball. I craved a change of conversation."

Stansbury sipped a glass of wine. "Don't worry. The day after tomorrow it will be over, and she'll move on to discussing the next social affair."

"You love to torment me."

"I'm afraid you are a tormented soul no longer, my friend. Miss Foster has brought you into the light, where we all reap the rewards of your quick wit and charm."

"You're in a poetic mood. Does this have anything to do with the object of your affections?"

"Most assuredly so."

"You must be convinced she returns your ardor?"

"Indeed, I've heard confirmation from her sweet lips just today."

"Confess her name, Stansbury. Keep me in suspense no longer."

Stansbury drained his wine. "Have you any objection to my declaring my intentions toward Amelie?"

Dallas threw his head back and laughed. "I've never heard anything more ridiculous. Amelie views you like an elder brother."

"She does not, I assure you."

Stansbury's usually merry countenance was deadly seri

ous, and Dallas suddenly realized his friend wasn't joking. "Hang on…aren't you in love with someone else?"

"Amelie has been the only woman in my thoughts for some time now."

Shock made Dallas sit upright. "Do you mean to say you've been courting my sister behind my back?"

"Hardly."

"Under my nose, then."

"Come now, Kirkendale. Amelie is a raging beauty. Can you be so surprised I might have noticed?"

"Yes, I can. This is positively absurd. You've known my sister practically since she was born."

"She's not a schoolgirl anymore!"

"That's beside the point!"

Dallas and Stansbury glared at one another. Finally, Stansbury rose. "If she doesn't marry me, then it will be some other lucky chap. You'd best get used to the idea you can't hold on to Amelie forever."

Stansbury lifted his chin and strode from the room. Dallas drank the rest of his whisky, trying to make sense of his conflicted thoughts. It pained him to quarrel with his closest friend, but the notion Stansbury had formed a romantic attachment to Dallas's sister was unpalatable. *Stansbury and Amelie in love? Impossible.*

At breakfast with Amelie the next morning, Dallas said nothing about his conversation with Stansbury. His sister seemed unaccountably nervous, biting her lip and flicking glances in his direction. Although he realized he was being curmudgeonly and possibly even unfair, he was reluctant to broach the topic. Usually he'd have the excuse of reading the morning paper to keep him occupied, but for some reason it had not been brought out with his food. He rang for his butler, who appeared shortly thereafter. "Mr. DeVane, I am missing my paper this morning."

"Pardon me, milord, but one of the footmen burned a hole in it with an iron. I sent him out to fetch a new one."

"I'll look forward to reading it later then."

After the butler left, Amelie cleared her throat. "Did you and Stansbury enjoy yourselves last night?"

"I can't say that we did." Dallas fixed her with his gaze. "He has the most peculiar idea you view him as a suitor. I set him straight, of course."

Amelie's complexion grew pale. "You didn't!"

"Stansbury has no right to impose himself on a girl too young to know her own mind."

"Don't be such an ass."

"Amelie!"

"Jessamine is scarcely a year older than I am, yet you see no problem imposing yourself on her!"

"That's different. I haven't known her all my life."

"It's only different because it suits your purpose! Perhaps you and Jessamine were attracted to one another right away, but that's not the only way a relationship begins. Fitzie and I have grown to care deeply for one another over the last year."

"*Fitzie*, is it? Have you considered that by marrying Stansbury, you would be marrying down? He's the youngest son of a Marquess, with little hope of inheriting the title!"

"Nevertheless, he owns considerable property and his income is more than ample to meet our needs. And since I'm not to inherit the earldom, I believe we're well matched."

Dallas folded his arms across his chest. "I want the best for you, Amelie."

"Fitzie is the best man I've ever met and you know it. May

the devil take you if you stand in our way." To her credit, Amelie didn't storm from the room. She folded her napkin, laid it on the table, and rose from her chair. "You will come around, Dallas. Of this, I have no doubt."

Astonished, he watched her leave the dining room with her head held high. *When did my little sister grow up?*

Bubbling with excitement, Jessamine watched Hannah carry a long fabric bag into her room and lay it gently across the bed. As Hannah unwrapped the bag, revealing the gown inside, Jessamine let out a slow breath. "Mademoiselle LaGrange insisted on so many alterations, I was beginning to worry it wouldn't be here in time for Amelie's ball tomorrow night."

The gossamer fabric of the white gown was accented with silken pink ribbons, and the skirt fell in a sumptuous arrangements of knife-pleated chiffon billowing out at the hem.

"Oh, Miss Jessamine! I'm not certain if I've ever seen anything so lovely. You'll be the most beautiful girl at the ball."

"Amelie is to wear Mama's debutante dress, so all eyes will be on her. I hope, however, I have *one* particular gentleman watching me."

Hannah jumped as the telephone downstairs began its plaintiff wail. "I can't get used to that horrible sound! It reminds me of a fire alarm."

"I tend to agree. One wonders what message could be so critical that it couldn't be sent by messenger." Jessamine shrugged. "I suppose we ought not be so old-fashioned."

Over the next few minutes they discussed which shoes, jewelry, gloves, and hair ornament would coordinate with the gown. Their conversation was interrupted by several additional phone calls. Jessamine and Hannah exchanged a surprised glance.

"That's odd, don't you think? I've been here over a fortnight and the telephone has not rung more than once per day, if that," Jessamine said.

"I'll go see if anything's amiss."

When Hannah opened the door, a man's voice, raised in anger, could be heard coming from the floor below. *Uncle Thackery is home, and he doesn't seem happy.* The maid cast a worried glance over her shoulder before disappearing downstairs. To Jessamine's surprise, Hannah returned immediately. After the briefest of knocks, she burst into the room—startling Jessamine into dropping a hair ornament.

"You're wanted in the drawing room immediately." Hannah lowered her voice. "Mr. and Mrs. Foster are horribly angry."

Jessamine's eyes widened. "Why?"

"I don't know, but the last time I saw them so stirred up, it had something to do with your aunt."

BEWILDERED, Jessamine made her way to the drawing room, where the air was heavy with tension. A florid-faced Mr. Foster was pacing near the fireplace and her aunt was nearly prostrate on the sofa. Only Charlotte, sitting in the window seat, wore a smirk. When Jessamine drew near, Mrs. Foster rolled to her feet and flew at her in a rage.

"You spawn of sin!" she shrieked. "You've brought ruin and disgrace to the Fosters. You're a slattern just like your mother!"

Has Aunt Rachel lost her mind? Jessamine forced herself to remain calm. "I'm well aware of your hatred for me, but I didn't realize it extended to my mother. Since she was the most virtuous of women, your slander is shocking."

"She means your *real* mother," Charlotte drawled. "The infamous prostitute, Paris Lilly."

Jessamine's jaw dropped. *My cousin has lost her mind too!* "Who?"

"Lillian Perrisham, otherwise known as the Paris Lilly," Charlotte replied.

Mr. Foster picked up a folded newspaper from the mantle and thrust it under her nose.

"According to a series of letters written by Lillian Perrisham to Minerva Foster, you are her natural daughter, raised by my brother and his wife."

Dizziness swept over Jessamine as she stared uncomprehendingly at the newspaper.

"That's just not possible."

"I let you stay at Arbor Manor because I thought you were my blood relative." Mr. Foster's tone quivered with barely restrained fury. "And I only took you back because your shrewish birth mother harangued and threatened me. Now, on the eve of Charlotte's debut, this scandal threatens to swamp her future. You've made a fool of me and I want you out of this house *now*."

"Where am I to go?"

"That's not my problem."

Mr. Foster grabbed Jessamine by the upper arm and dragged her through the house toward the front door.

"Let me go, Uncle Thackery! At least allow me to get my coat!"

"I'm not your uncle!"

The ruckus brought servants on the run. As they looked on, wide-eyed, Mr. Foster opened the front door, shoved Jessamine through it, and slammed it shut.

CHAPTER 13

REVELATIONS

With no coat, gloves, or hat, Jessamine stood outside the Fosters' townhouse for a long time, braving the curious looks of passersby. It was as if the shock had filled her mind with cotton and she did not have the ability to form a thought. Blood pounded in her ears, and an uncontrollable tremor shook her hands. Although she longed to run to Dallas's townhouse, she didn't dare. *I cannot bear to tell him I'm the natural daughter of a prostitute. I'm not worthy to be his wife, must less work as a companion to his sister!* Eventually, she edged away from the house and wandered down the street. *Perhaps if I sit awhile in St. Peter's Church, I can collect myself. Surely I'm still welcome in God's house!*

"Wait! Miss Jessamine, wait!"

Hannah ran down the sidewalk toward her, clad in a sensible dark coat. She clutched Jessamine's reticule in her hand and carried a lightweight mantle over her arm. When the maid caught up with Jessamine, she draped the mantle around her shoulders.

"Thank you," Jessamine murmured. "I hope your kindness doesn't get you into trouble with the Fosters."

"I don't care about their opinion one way or another. I've quit their employ to come with you."

"I've nowhere to go, Hannah, and no money. You'd best return to the Fosters and ask them to take you back."

"I'm not going to leave you. Do you want to stay with Lord Kirkendale and his sister?"

"No! If what my uncle—Mr. Foster—says is true, I don't want this scandal to taint Amelie."

"I thought you might feel that way." Hannah reached into Jessamine's reticule and retrieved Lillian Perrisham's calling card. "Miss Perrisham will know what to do. She's a good woman, despite her reputation."

Hannah waved down a hansom cab, ushered Jessamine inside, and directed the driver to Mayfair. As the cab rolled forward, Jessamine dropped her face into her hands and dissolved into silent, helpless tears. Hannah comforted her as best she could.

"The Fosters are evil people, if you don't mind me saying so," she said finally.

"I don't mind you saying so. Not in the least."

LILLY THRUST a tot of brandy into Jessamine's hands and made her drink it. As the strong liquid burned her throat, Jessamine shuddered. Nevertheless, the ensuing numbness and warmth was welcome. After Lilly refilled her glass, Jessamine drank that down too. Her vision grew blurred from the tears welling up in her eyes.

"When I first saw the newspaper story, I called the Fosters

right away," Lilly said. "Mr. Foster told me you refused to come to the telephone."

"That's nonsense," Hannah said.

Jessamine fixed her watery gaze on Lilly. "Is the newspaper story true?"

"Yes." Lilly poured an additional two tots of brandy, gave one to Hannah, and drank the other herself. "I was young and foolish when Minerva and I made our debut. We were seen as first-class beauties in a sea of pretty girls."

"I saw a photograph of you together," Jessamine said. "You were both extraordinary."

"As time went on, Minerva went about her life in the traditional way and married Jesse Foster. But I allowed the flattery and compliments to go to my head like too much brandy. I went to Paris and met a man. Soon thereafter, I discovered I was with child."

Wide-eyed, Hannah flushed red and gulped down her brandy.

"My long-suffering parents were angry and I didn't blame them," Lilly continued. "After they washed their hands of me, Minerva came to my rescue. By that time, she'd discovered she was unable to bear children. She and Jesse agreed to pass you off as their own daughter."

"I can't believe it," Jessamine murmured. "I had no idea."

"You were born in Paris. Afterward, the four of us traveled to Arbor Manor, where a brand new staff had been hired to prevent any inconvenient gossip. I stayed with you for several weeks, but Minerva finally gave me an ultimatum; if you were to be her daughter, I would have to leave and never have contact with you again." Tears filled Lilly's eyes and spilled down her cheeks. "I returned to France, where I became the Paris Lilly." She smiled through her tears. "At least my life has not been boring."

"I suppose that explains why Papa set aside no assets for me from the estate," Jessamine said. "I wasn't really his daughter."

"You were his daughter in all the ways that mattered, Jessamine. He loved you dearly, but since he knew you were my flesh and blood, I think he was concerned any sizable bequest might be investigated by his lawyer and the scandal revealed."

"And the man who is my real father? Your letters only referred to him as Mr. X."

"And as Mr. X he shall remain. I'm sorry, dearest, but that's the way it must be for now."

"I'd like to know how the newspaper got hold of those letters," Jessamine said. "I left a bundle of them in Mama's box of keepsakes back at Arbor Manor."

"Miss Charlotte was always snooping in your room, that's how," Hannah said. "She must have stolen them...just like Mrs. Foster stole your letters from Miss Perrisham."

"Mr. Foster will soon discover he ought not to have crossed me," Lilly said.

"What are you going to do?" Jessamine asked.

"I'm calling a policeman of my acquaintance about a theft."

THE FOSTERS HAD ASSEMBLED in the dining room for lunch. Mr. Foster peered at the middle-aged, apron-clad woman as she brought in a tureen of soup. "Mrs. Pool, why are you serving? Are we short-handed in the kitchen?"

"Aye, sir. The staff is in uproar, I'm afraid."

"What seems to be the problem?" Mrs. Foster asked.

"There's a bit of resentment over Miss Jessamine's abrupt departure."

"That's ridiculous," Mrs. Foster replied. "I'll take the staff in hand after lunch."

"Er…yes, madam." The cook removed her apron. "I'm afraid you'll have to bring the rest of the meal to the table yourselves."

"What? That's outrageous," Mrs. Foster said.

"Yes, Mrs. Foster, but I've a family emergency to attend to. There's no way of knowing when I'll be back."

As the woman ambled from the room, the Fosters gaped at one another.

"Mrs. Pool has no family of which I am aware," Mrs. Foster said, bewildered.

"Of course not. Nor does she intend to return," Mr. Foster replied.

Charlotte lifted the lid of the tureen, and gasped. "It's empty!"

Mr. Foster's face turned a mottled color. "Heads will roll for this." He rang for the butler, but Mr. Hattley didn't respond. "I believe we have a mutiny on hand."

"I'm hungry!" Charlotte wailed.

Mr. Foster tossed his napkin onto the table and stood. "I'm going to my club for lunch. Sort this out by the time I return, Mrs. Foster."

He strode out. Just as the door slammed, the phone began to ring again. Charlotte pushed her chair back. "I'll get it."

"No, don't," Mrs. Foster said. "If it's about the newspaper story, I'd rather not talk to anyone about it just now. Perhaps by tomorrow, things will blow over."

"What are we going to do about lunch?"

"Let's you and I go downstairs to eat. I'll have to ring up the employment agency this afternoon and hire a new cook and butler."

When they went downstairs, however, Charlotte and her mother discovered the kitchen and staff dining room were empty, and the oven was cool.

"Mrs. Pool was lying," Charlotte said. "Nothing's been cooked at all!"

"We're going to need a whole new staff, it seems."

"I'm *starving*, Mama."

"Go into the pantry and find some bread and cheese," Mrs. Foster said. "I'll put on the tea kettle and slice some fruit."

After a little exploration, Charlotte located the pantry and gathered together a half-loaf of bread, a crock of butter, cheese, a jar of pickles, and a crock of marmalade. She and her mother made a picnic in the staff dining hall.

Mrs. Foster gave Charlotte a bright smile. "This isn't so bad. It's sort of like the old days."

"We still had servants in the old days," Charlotte retorted. "And we always kept a cook."

"I should have restaffed when we first moved into Arbor Manor," Mrs. Foster said. "Otherwise there's no way to know where a servant's loyalty lies."

Sullen and out of sorts, Charlotte gnawed on a crust of bread and butter. As she chewed, her thoughts wandered to Jessamine's room. Suddenly her mood brightened.

"You look as if you've a bee in your bonnet," Mrs. Foster said.

"I just remembered all the gowns Jessamine had delivered from La Mad Modiste!" Charlotte exclaimed. "To the victor belong the spoils."

CHARLOTTE STOOD outside Jessamine's room and kicked the door in frustration. "It's locked!"

A crease of annoyance formed on Mrs. Foster's brow. "That awful Hannah must've locked it for spite. Go to the housekeeper's office and get her ring of keys."

"Oh, bother."

Propelled by her desire to see what treasures lay on the other side of Jessamine's door, Charlotte practically flew down two flights of stairs. Movement in the servant's dining hall startled her into stopping flat. "Who's there?"

A young man's earnest face appeared. "It's me, Eugene. Pardon me, Miss Charlotte, but do you know where everyone got off to? I went out to fetch something and when I come back the staff had disappeared."

"They walked out and left us without any help at all. It's all Jessamine's fault."

Eugene gaped. "Well that's just not right, is it?"

"No, it's *not*."

The doorbell rang. Charlotte bit her lip. *I can't answer my own door! What if it's one of my friends...or a gentleman caller!* "Go answer the door, Eugene."

"But I'm not the butler!"

"You are now."

The doorbell rang again, and Eugene hastened off. Charlotte searched in the housekeeper's office, but when she located the key ring her smile of triumph was brief. *There must be fifty keys at least!*

A murmur of loud conversation upstairs alerted her to visitors. Mrs. Foster's shriek of dismay brought Charlotte running. When she reached the entrance hall, a policeman was hauling her mother from the house, another officer was pacing near a potted palm, and Hannah was leading a pair of liveried footmen up the stairs. Eugene was standing against the wall, bewildered.

"What's happening!" Charlotte exclaimed.

The remaining policeman stopped pacing. "Miss Charlotte Foster? We've a warrant for the arrest of your mother on charges of theft. She's been taken into custody until the hearing."

"But—"

"Hannah is retrieving her personal property and that of Miss Jessamine Foster from the premises," the officer concluded.

In a daze, Charlotte could only stare in dismay as the footmen carried a parade of finery from Jessamine's room. When it was over, the policeman and footmen left while Hannah dropped the key to Jessamine's bedroom into the palm of Charlotte's hand.

"Have a lovely day, Miss Foster."

The front door slammed, and Charlotte burst into tears. After a moment, Eugene shuffled over and patted her arm. "You'll be all right, Miss Charlotte. Maybe I can fix you a cup of tea?"

"Oh, Eugene!" Charlotte launched herself into the man's arms and sobbed.

STINGING from his recent quarrels with Stansbury and Amelie, Dallas went riding alone in Hyde Park. Nothing had been the same since Jessamine left. He missed seeing her every morning at breakfast and evening before bed. At the moment, he longed to ask her advice about Amelie. *I'll walk to the Fosters after lunch and pay her a call. Jessamine always finds a way to set my mind at ease.* With that decided, he returned home in a slightly better mood.

His good humor evaporated, however, when he noticed Stansbury's carriage parked out front. Dallas walked into the house and spied Amelie and Stansbury in the drawing room, locked in an embrace. He strode over and pulled the two of them apart.

"You're not welcome in this house when I'm not present, Stansbury!"

Dallas was alarmed to discover traces of tears on his sister's face. Just as he clenched his fist to knock Stansbury flat, Amelie grabbed his arm. "Stop, Dallas. It's Jessamine! She's in trouble."

Concern and distress were etched on Stansbury's face. "Haven't you read the paper today? There's a horrible scandal involving poor Miss Foster." Stansbury grabbed a folded newspaper from a nearby table and thrust it into Dallas's hands.

A chill, bordering on panic, ran down Dallas's spine as he read the article. A wave of dizziness swept over him, and he was forced to sit afterward. Bile rose up in his throat when he recalled the final part of his conversation with his attorney, Mr. Oatley.

"And does my father's mistress still live?"

"Yes, she moved from Paris to London years ago. Her name is Lillian Perrisham."

Aghast, Dallas tore his gaze from the newspaper and stared at Amelie. If the article was correct, Jessamine was her sister. And if his father had also sired Jessamine, she was his half-sister too.

"Dallas, are you all right? You suddenly look quite ill," Stansbury said.

"I'm fine," he managed. *Nothing could be further from the truth.*

❧

Lilly showed Jessamine upstairs to a bright and pretty bedchamber with a sitting room and an adjoining bath.

"This is lovely." Jessamine gave Lilly a wan smile. "Thank you for taking me in. I'm not sure what I would have done otherwise."

"I wish you hadn't found out the truth this way, but I'm very happy you're here. When you're ready, perhaps we can make plans for the future. We could spend time at my country estate if you like, or maybe you'd prefer to go abroad?"

At the thought of leaving Dallas and Amelie, Jessamine lost her composure completely. Lilly led her to one of the sitting room chairs and sat with her until her sobbing eased.

"Lady Amelie's debut ball is tomorrow night," Jessamine said. "I must send my regrets I'll be unable to attend."

A wistful expression came over Lilly's face. "Tell me about her."

"Amelie's a wonderful girl, extremely pretty, and has a generous nature. She doesn't lack for accomplishments, either. She plays the piano, is an excellent horsewoman, and she speaks French like a native."

"You two are quite close?"

"She's almost like a sister. She's to wear Mama's—*Minerva's*—debutante dress tomorrow night."

"Please don't think of Minerva any other way than your Mama. She adored you." Lilly paused. "And what of Lady Amelie's brother?"

"Lord Kirkendale is very handsome." Jessamine's throat closed up and she shook her head, unable to continue. *I will never see him again and I can't bear it.*

"I daresay he favors his father. I knew Phillip Marsden in Paris...a lifetime ago." A sigh escaped Lilly's lips. "Why don't you lie down and rest a while? It may be some time until Hannah and my footmen return with your luggage."

Emotionally spent, Jessamine took her advice and crawled onto the bed. Lilly crossed over to the windows, drew the curtains, and snapped off the electric lights.

"Try to sleep, Jessamine," she murmured. "I believe everything will be all right in the end."

Jessamine was left alone with her thoughts until exhaustion and brandy led her to sleep.

CHAPTER 14

TRUTH AND CONSEQUENCES

Dallas dragged himself out of his emotional tailspin. *Now is not the time to reflect how this scandal affects me personally. It's Jessamine who is suffering the most, and I must go to her.*

"I need to see Jessamine," he said. *Then I'll visit Miss Perrisham to learn the truth.*

"I rang the Fosters after Fitzie brought me the news, but nobody answered the telephone," Amelie said. "I don't know if anyone's home."

"I can't imagine the Fosters would be out and about, given the circumstances," Stansbury said. "They are likely not answering the telephone."

"I'll walk over there right now," Dallas said. "I've no appetite for lunch anyway."

"Neither do I. Let me get my coat and I'll go with you," Amelie said.

"No. I wish to speak with Jessamine alone." He ignored Amelie's pout, turned toward Stansbury, and extended his hand. "No hard feelings? I misunderstood the purpose of your visit and should have given you the benefit of the doubt just now. Please forgive me."

The two men exchanged a handshake.

"No hard feelings." Stansbury picked up his hat. "I'll take my leave, but please call me after you've spoken with Miss Foster. This can't be a pleasant turn of events for her."

"I cannot imagine what Jessamine's going through," Amelie said. "I think I should die if I discovered my parents weren't actually my parents."

Dallas winced inwardly. "I'm sure it's a horrible shock for her, but she's resilient."

"I expect Jessamine will come through this with the help of her friends." Stansbury reached for Amelie's hand and gave it a reassuring squeeze. "I, for one, shall not abandon her."

"Nor shall I. Jessamine has more friends than she realizes," Amelie replied.

As Stansbury and Amelie exchanged a radiant smile, Dallas frowned. *My sister truly loves him.*

DALLAS STRODE TOWARD THE FOSTERS' townhouse, where two footmen were loading trunks from the sidewalk onto the luggage rack of a large carriage. Dallas recognized the trunks as Jessamine's. He glanced inside the carriage, but except for several hatboxes it was empty. A policeman emerged from the Fosters' residence, followed shortly thereafter by Hannah. *What's a policeman doing here?* His mouth went dry at the thought of any harm befalling Jessamine. The officer tipped his hat at Hannah and then ambled off toward the horse tethered to a hitching post nearby.

"Pardon me, Hannah, but is Miss Jessamine all right?" Dallas asked.

She regarded him with sad eyes. "You've read the paper, I suppose?"

"Indeed I have, and I must see her."

"Miss Jessamine doesn't live with the Fosters any longer, but I'm not at liberty to say where she's gone."

"Please tell me. My sister and I only want to reassure her of our continued friendship. I won't rest until I've spoken with her."

Hannah chewed her lower lip as she studied him. He did his best not to seem desperate, but it was a losing battle.

"Milord, I'm sorry, but she's been through a great deal," she said finally. "I'll let her know you wish to see her."

"If you don't tell me where she is, I'll follow this carriage on foot if I must," he said. "I'm quite determined."

The woman made a sound of exasperation. "I suppose I've already broken all notions of protocol anyway, so what does one more transgression matter? You may ride along with me if you don't mind holding a few hatboxes. I can't guarantee Miss Jessamine will see you."

"Where is she?"

"The less said about that on a public sidewalk, the better. Let's go."

DALLAS DID his best not to explode as Hannah described how Mr. Foster had forcibly expelled Jessamine from his abode that morning without so much as a wrap.

"How utterly despicable," he said, seething. "I'll throttle the man."

"The entire staff up and quit in protest—except for Eugene, apparently."

"I'm glad to hear it. Mr. Foster does not deserve to be called a gentleman."

"He'll get his just desserts when he discovers his wife was arrested for stealing the money Miss Perrisham sent Miss Jessamine over the years. Now *that's* a scandal people won't soon forget."

"H-How is Jessamine?" A stab of anxiety shot through him..

"I've never seen the poor lamb look so lost as she did after Mr. Foster threw her into the street—not even when she left Arbor Manor. Miss Perrisham was ever so gracious to take the both of us in. Despite the woman's past, I won't hear an unkind word about her."

"You won't get an argument from me," Dallas replied. "I saw her once, when I was out riding. She drew nearly as much excitement as a member of the royal family."

"Aye, she's that handsome, even though she's no longer a young girl. If you saw Miss Jessamine and Miss Perrisham side-by-side, there's no denying the resemblance."

"I'd rather she be related to the Paris Lilly than the Fosters."

Lilly's breath caught in her throat at the sight of the young earl waiting in her drawing room. Although the butler had presented her with the visitor's calling card, she would have known the gentleman anywhere. *Lord Kirkendale bears an uncanny resemblance to his father.* He stood as she entered the room, concern etched on his handsome features. *Not so much like Phillip after all. This man has a warm heart.*

"Miss Perrisham, my name is Dallas Marsden, the seventh earl of Kirkendale."

"It's a pleasure to meet you, Lord Kirkendale. I expect you're here about Jessamine?"

"Is she all right?"

"As well as can be expected, although she's had rather a shock. She's resting, but I'll ask her if she feels up to visitors."

"I would prefer to have a word with you in utmost privacy first, if I may."

Lilly raised one eyebrow, but moved to close the drawing room doors before taking a seat on the sofa.

"Miss Perrisham, for nearly eighteen years my family has been blackmailed by Sir Bartholomew Hightower. Until recently, I didn't know the exact reason why. I sought the advice of my father's attorney, and he informed me that my sister is actually the natural daughter born to my father and his mistress, Lillian Perrisham."

"I see."

"If you're Jessamine's birth mother, it's critical for me to know…" Kirkendale took a deep breath and his hands were visibly trembling. "Was my father also her sire?"

"Why is this important to you?"

"Because I love Jessamine. I wish with all my heart to make her my wife. Please relieve my suffering and tell me the truth."

"You are not related to Jessamine whatsoever."

Kirkendale closed his eyes and bowed his head. "Thank God."

"Nor is Lady Amelie my daughter."

His head snapped up. "What?"

"She's your full-blooded sibling, milord. As it so happens, your mother and I were carrying Phillip's children at the same time, and gave birth within weeks of one another. Unfortunately, my daughter was stillborn."

"I'm awfully sorry."

"Thank you. Bart knew about my confinement and used it to blackmail Phillip."

"This is very confusing. How did Bart come to believe Amelie was yours?"

"Your mother had an affair early in her marriage, and Phillip never forgave her for it. He suspected, unfairly, Lady Amelie was the result of another illicit liaison. Rather than sully Jacqueline's reputation, Phillip let Bart believe Amelie was mine. Since I loved him, I kept his secret until now."

"My father lied to his own attorney to keep up the charade?"

"Although he enjoyed the intrigue and drama, Phillip loved Lady Amelie and didn't want her hurt. He also held Bart's blackmail over your mother's head, to punish her for having taken a lover."

"You make him sound wicked."

"Phillip was a fallible human being, perhaps more easily led by his passions than most. I loved him, but I was not faithful either. We were both quite similar in many ways."

"Who was Jessamine's father?"

Lilly smiled. "On that subject, I shall keep my own counsel. The only thing that's important is she's no kin of yours."

STILL SLIGHTLY BLEARY-EYED from her nap, Jessamine watched Hannah direct the footmen where to place her trunks. "And put the rest in the room down the hall, lads."

The footmen left, and the maid turned to face Jessamine. "I have my work cut out for me. I packed your gowns in such a hurry I must unpack them this afternoon before they become too crushed."

"Thank you so much," Jessamine said. "Did the Fosters give you any trouble?"

"Not at all. Mr. Foster was absent when I arrived, and Mrs. Foster was taken to the police station. Miss Charlotte was shocked, but since this was her doing, I don't feel sorry for her."

Lilly tapped on the door. "Jessamine, dear, you have a gentleman caller downstairs. It's Lord Kirkendale."

"What?" Jessamine's hands flew to her hair, which was unpinned and hanging to her waist. "I'm not properly dressed to see him!"

"You look perfect just as you are." Lilly crossed into the room and pulled Jessamine's hair forward and over one shoulder. "Trust me, it won't do Lord Kirkendale any harm to see you vulnerable and in need of his protection."

"Lilly!"

Hannah was bent double as she unpacked a trunk, but even so Jessamine could hear her giggle.

"How did he know I was here?" Jessamine's accusing glance rested on the maid.

"Er...His Lordship showed up just as I was leaving the Fosters and threatened to make a public scene if I didn't let him come with me in the carriage." Hannah shrugged. "What else could I do?"

Jessamine averted her eyes. "I'd hoped to break things off with a letter. I suppose that makes me a coward."

"His Lordship is in the drawing room," Lilly said. "Don't keep him waiting."

~

As she descended the stairs, Jessamine gripped the rail as if it were a lifeline. She wished she had time to rehearse what she should say. *I must relieve Dallas of any sense of obligation and convey my gratitude for his former friendship.* Despite her vow to remain calm, Jessamine paused at the foot of the stairs to blot tears away with her handkerchief. Afterward, she straightened her shoulders and entered the drawing room.

Dallas shot to his feet when she appeared, his golden hair glinting in the light from the chandelier. Although her thoughts instantly became jumbled, she was determined to do the proper thing.

"It's very kind of you to call, Lord Kirkendale." Her voice quavered, but she strengthened her resolve and plunged forward. "I want you and Lady Amelie to know how grateful I am for your friendship. My relationship with Lilly has altered everything, however, and it would be unseemly for us to continue our acquaintance."

She paused, waiting for his reply, but he seemed unable to speak.

"With your permission, I-I'll write a letter to your sister. I-I do apologize for any embarrassment or discomfort this episode has caused you..."

With a sob, she whirled around to flee, but Dallas caught her in his arms and held her close. As she cried, he whispered soothing words of comfort.

"Now see here, nothing has changed between us," he said. "Never doubt how much I love and adore you. If you're agreeable, I'm going to announce our engagement at Amelie's debutante ball tomorrow night."

"Oh, Dallas, you can't! Don't you understand what damage will be done to her chances to make a suitable marriage?"

"It seems the matter has already been decided." He chuckled. "Stansbury and Amelie are in love."

Jessamine gasped. "Really? Well, I suppose it's not surprising, now that I think about it. I suspected her partiality almost right away."

"Why didn't you say anything?"

"I was too busy fighting my attraction to you."

He captured her lips and made her forget everything except the warmth of his body and the delicious melting sensations arising within.

"I'll send the carriage for you and Miss Perrisham tomorrow night," he murmured.

Jessamine stepped back, aghast. "Have you lost your mind?"

"Since she is to be my future mother-in-law, I'd like her to attend. Besides which, the presence of the Paris Lilly will create quite a stir, don't you think? Society will talk of nothing else for months."

With a contented sigh, Jessamine relaxed into Dallas's embrace once more.

"You really *are* mad...but I love you."

As the carriage came to a halt outside the banquet hall the following evening, Jessamine shot a terrified glance at Lilly. "I don't think I can do this. What if everyone stares or makes snide comments?"

"People *will* stare and some will make snide comments. They would have done so in any case, but the scandal gives them a comfortable excuse to behave in an uncharitable manner. Make no mistake, nobody lives a blameless life. Many people love to point fingers at others, hoping no one will notice their own flaws."

"How can you be so fearless?"

"I'm not fearless, but I know who has skeletons in their closets. Such knowledge is a superior weapon when the witty battle the witless."

Lilly was clad in magnificent Charles Worth ball gown in deep sapphire, with feather appliqués across the bodice and down the skirt. Jessamine wore a high collared evening cape in pearlescent taffeta, which covered her borrowed debutante dress of snowy white tulle. Hannah had woven strings of pearls into her hair and arranged most of it high on her crown. The remainder was fashioned into a cascade of lustrous curls down her back.

The carriage door opened, and a footman extended his hand to Jessamine. She stepped out and waited for Lilly, to no avail. The beautiful woman merely leaned forward and gave her daughter a smile. "Have a lovely time, darling."

"What! Aren't you coming with me?"

"Tonight the focus should be on you and Lady Amelie Marsden. Give Lord Kirkendale my regrets and tell him I have a dinner engagement to attend."

Before Jessamine could protest, the carriage door shut and the vehicle rolled forward. She had no choice but to move into the hall, relinquish her cape to an attendant, and receive her dance card. By design she'd arrived late, to slip into the ball as unobtrusively as possible. The dancing had not yet begun, however, and guests were sipping punch and chatting in small groups. No familiar faces presented themselves, although a great many gentlemen gave her frank looks of appreciation. As Jessamine passed a trio of young ladies, a sneering voice rang out.

"If it's not the governess!" Olivia exclaimed. "Henrietta and Mildred, meet Miss Jessamine Foster, the Paris Lilly's secret daughter."

Gasps ensued.

"*You're* the Paris Lilly's daughter?" Henrietta asked Jessamine. "What's she like?"

"I heard she won't use anything but spun gold thread on her gowns," Mildred said. "Is that true?"

Jessamine stifled a smile at Olivia's expression of disgust and disappointment.

"Lillian Perrisham is a lovely, warm woman with a marvelous sense of style," Jessamine replied. "I can't tell you about the thread, but I can tell you of her kindness."

Dallas appeared, searching for someone in the crowd. *He is looking for me.* When his gaze locked with Jessamine's, his dazzling smile nearly took her breath away. *The man grows more handsome with every passing moment.* Jessamine excused herself and hastened to join him. *It matters little if I am accepted by strangers so long as I'm loved by friends.*

As Lilly was ushered through the fashionable restaurant, heads turned and tongues began to wag. In the back of the establishment were several private rooms, where intimate dinners for two often took place. The maître d'hôtel took Lilly's cape and opened the very last door for her. She stilled the trembling of her hands and entered the room, mustering every iota of poise in her possession. A formally-attired older man of substantial girth stood near the fireplace, staring into the flames as if deep in thought. At her arrival he glanced up and gave her a sad smile. She sank into a curtsy.

"Your Majesty."

"Lillian, it's uncommonly good to see you after all these years."

On the table, two glasses of champagne had already been poured. He handed one to her, and leaned in to give Lilly an impulsive kiss on the cheek. They drank a silent toast, during which a thousand unspoken emotions seemed to dart back and forth between them. Finally, the king lowered his glass and took Lilly's hand.

"Why did you never tell me we had a daughter?"

The End

After Mrs. Rachel Foster's arrest became public, Mr. Foster spent increasingly longer periods of time with his mistress. A judge ultimately found Mrs. Foster guilty of grand larceny and sent her to jail for a period of several weeks. Testimony from Eugene the footman was instrumental in her conviction, and he was discharged from his employment as a result.

Charlotte Foster's Season was a disaster. After Mrs. Foster was released from jail, she and Charlotte left London and returned to Arbor Manor in disgrace. Mr. Foster stayed behind in the Eaton Square townhouse with his mistress and a brand new staff. He was forced to travel to Arbor Manor, however, when it was discovered Charlotte was in the family way. With considerable effort, Mr. Foster located the child's father, Eugene, at his family's farm in Cornwall. After thrashing Eugene soundly, Mr. Foster suffered a fatal heart attack. Arbor Manor and the entire estate was entailed away from Mrs. Foster and Charlotte, and came into the possession of a distant American cousin by the name of Frederick Foster. Charlotte married Eugene, and moved into his modest four-room house with Mrs. Foster and his parents.

Sir Bartholomew Hightower and Lady Hightower sold their homes in Kent and London, and moved to a small house in Newcastle. Although Sir Bart spent most of his time thereafter in a drunken stupor, Lady Hightower opened a small tea shop which managed to stay profitable. Olivia Hightower gave up looking for a husband and took a job with a London newspaper as a Society news columnist. In spring of 1912, she was given a plum assignment to cover the maiden launch of a luxury passenger liner heading to New York City from Southampton.

Since the passenger list contained the names of many extremely wealthy men, Olivia boarded the *RMS Titanic* with lingering hopes of cultivating a romantic relationship with one of them. Unfortunately, the ship hit an iceberg four days into the crossing, and Olivia perished.

As Amelie predicted, Dallas came around to the idea of her marriage to Stansbury. He did, however, insist on a year-long engagement, despite his sister calling him "mulish." La Mad Modiste created Amelie's wedding dress, photos of which appeared in the newspaper. The design became a sensation. With Lillian Perrisham's financial backing, Mademoiselle Madeleine LeGrange opened up exclusive dress shops in Paris and Manhattan the following year. Lillian designed a popular line of gowns for La Mad Modiste, under the label Paris Lilly.

Dallas obtained a special license so he and Jessamine could marry quickly. As a gift to his new bride, Dallas discharged most of his Knight's Keep staff and replaced them with as many of Arbor Manor's former servants as possible. Jessamine made friends with Arbor Manor's new owner, Frederick Foster, who gifted her with her family portrait recovered from the attic. She and Frederick, a writer, became friends. Frederick took an unusual shine to Hannah, and the two eventually married. Lillian never disclosed the identity of Jessamine's real father. After King Edward VII's death in 1910, however, Jessamine discovered the monarch had bequeathed her a large amount of money. Despite the bequest, King Edward never acknowledged Jessamine as his daughter, and their blood relationship never became publicly known.

SNEAK PEEK AT THE GLASS HEART

After Merrill's widowed mother becomes engaged to an earl, the fate of their respective estates hangs in the balance. A battle of wits ensues when the earl's arrogant son shows up to make demands. Despite their prickly start, once Merrill discovers she and the viscount have both been painfully crossed in love, she begins to feel a measure of empathy. Unfortunately for their burgeoning relationship, a tempestuous drama threatens to tear them apart forever.

Keep reading for an excerpt...

Excerpt from *The Glass Heart*

When Merrill finally loosed her last arrow, it sank into the red center with a satisfying thwack. She was puzzled to discover the muscles in her arms and back were shaking, until she remembered she'd been practicing for over three hours. She stretched out her arms as she strode toward the target to retrieve her arrows. "Practice makes perfect, as they say."

On her return, she noticed the portly butler approaching with an uncharacteristic frown on his face.

She cocked her head. "What is it, Northam?"

He presented a silver salver containing a card. "Lord Wharton has arrived."

"I've never heard of the man." Merrill peered at the engraved card made of heavy parchment, upon which was written, *The Right Honorable, The Viscount Wharton.* "What a bother." She dropped her arrows into the quiver stand and stripped off her leather arm guard. "I suppose I ought to receive him."

"Perhaps I should have said he intends to stay." Northam wore a pained expression. "He brought a considerable amount of luggage as well as his valet."

"What?" Merrill was taken aback. "That's absurd!"

Northam nodded. "I insisted nothing be unloaded from the carriage until I spoke to you."

"You did quite right. Ravenell is not a hotel, for mercy's sake."

Merrill lifted her chin as she strode toward the house. As she approached the drawing room, she was dismayed to hear the sound of piano music — a song from Gilbert and Sullivan's *The Gondoliers*

"Cheeky devil," she muttered.

Despite her irritation, Merrill plastered a serene smile to her lips as she sailed into the room. A young man was sitting at the baby grand piano and she was obliged to raise her voice to be heard. "Excuse me?"

Lord Wharton broke off playing and rose to his feet. "You must be Miss Cawthorne? Good afternoon." He picked up a snifter of amber liquid from the piano lid and lifted it up as if in a toast. "Thank you for making me feel welcome here at Ravenell."

Despite his words, the man's eyes glittered with obvious and inexplicable dislike.

"If I *have* made you feel welcome, it was entirely inadvertent." Merrill returned his glare with one of her own. "You've not been invited, so what is the meaning of this intrusion?"

"Forgive me but I *have* been invited — by your mother," With his left hand, Lord Wharton extricated a letter from his jacket pocket. "This letter of introduction is addressed to you."

As Merrill crossed the room to pluck the letter from his fingers, he swirled the amber liquid with appreciation. "I usually don't drink before dinner but this brandy is lovely."

She bristled. "It's Armagnac from Gascony, and it's a very rare vintage."

"Mmm." He took a long swallow. "*C'est magnifique.*"

Merrill discovered the letter was in her mother's hand and did indeed appear to be a letter of introduction. She read the entire missive through twice before glancing at her unwanted guest.

"You are Lord Seacombe's son, then." Merrill gritted her teeth. "I am to show you every courtesy."

Lord Wharton bowed. "I am delighted to meet you, Miss Cawthorne — or should I call you sister?"

"We are not related yet, so Miss Cawthorne will do." She peered at him. "Why have you come?"

He put the snifter down so hard she thought he might have broken the stem. "In contemplation of marriage to your mother, my father may sell his estate out from under me."

"That's unfortunate, sir, but what does that have to do with me?"

He fixed her with his gaze. "In contemplation of marriage to my father, your mother may sell Ravenell instead."

Merrill gasped. "What? No!"

"It will be one or the other. Neither my father nor your mother have decided yet."

"That's not possible."

"It is not only possible, but from what I overheard, they have indicated the sale of one estate is a certainty." Lord Wharton's eyes narrowed. "If we do not find a way to stop this travesty of a union, one of us will be deprived of our home."

About the Author

Originally from Southern California, Suzanne G. Rogers currently resides in beautiful Savannah, Georgia on an island populated by exotic birds, deer, turtles, otters, and gators.

HISTORICAL ROMANCE TITLES

Graceling Hall Series

Larken (Book One)*

Lord Apollo & the Colleen (Book Two)

The Vanishing Beauty (Book Three)

The Beaucroft Girls Series

Ruse & Romance (Book One)*

Rake & Romance (Book Two)*

The Mannequin Series

The Mannequin (Book One)*

Grace Unmasked (Book Two)

The Star-Crossed Seamstress (Book Three)

A Chance of Rayne (Book Four)

The Substitute (Book Five)

The Gilded Age Series

Duke of a Gilded Age (Book One)

Lady of a Gilded Age (Book Two)

Standalone Titles

A Gift for Fiona

*Spinster**

Lady Fallows' Secrets

*My Fair Guardian**

*Jessamine's Folly**

*The Ice Captain's Daughter**

Rumer Has It

An American in Paris of the West

Courtship on Eaton Square

The Prettier Sister

The Glass Heart

One Little Kiss

*Available in audiobook format

FANTASY TITLES

The Yden Series

The Last Great Wizard of Yden (Book One)

Dragon Clan of Yden (Book Two)

Secrets of Yden (Book Three)

Kira (Prequel to the Yden Series)

Standalone Titles

Dani & the Immortals

*The Dragon Rider's Daughter**

Clash of Wills

Tournament of Chance: Dragon Rebel

Magical Misperception

*Whimsical Tendencies**

Something Wicked in L.A.

Royal Promenade

**Audiobook Available*